I0761964

BREAKING THE CHAIN

A NOVEL BY

FRANKIE BERRY WISE

WISE Scholars Publishing

"We Bring Life to Learning"

First published by WISE Scholars Publishing, July 2013
(Second Edition published, May 2016)
Atlanta, Georgia USA 30318

10 9 8 7 6 5 4 3 2 1

www.wisescholarspublishing.com

Library of Congress Cataloging-in-Publication Data

Wise, Frankie Berry
Breaking the Chain

Summary: *Breaking the Chain* depicts the struggles of five mulatto women as they work through their relationships with each other and with the citizens of Crosstown, Georgia.

This fictional novel focuses on the Jackson women and how they, as individuals and as a unit, deal with many of their problems—including racial prejudice, socioeconomic disadvantages, molestation, infidelity, and death. *Breaking the Chain* gives a vivid and descriptive glimpse into the lives of these women as they attempt to preserve the chain that binds them.

Breaking the Chain has been adapted into a stage play entitled *Broken Promises*.

Paperback:
ISBN-13: 978-0615859545
ISBN-10: 0615859542

Hardback:
ISBN-13: 978-0-9963946-1-1
ISBN-10: 0996394613

Printed in the United States of America

Cover Design: Soweto Bosia, Blue Boy Media
Copy Editing: Dr. N. Jeff Carden, III
Substantive Editing: Marshalette R. Wise, WISE Scholars Publishing

DISCLAIMER: This is a work of fiction. Names, characters, businesses, places, events, and incidents are either the products of the author's imagination or used in a fictitious manner. Any resemblance to actual persons, living or dead, or actual events is purely coincidental.

FOREWORD

Frankie Berry Wise has been my friend and patient for almost three decades before she published her first book, *Exit*, in late 2012. In all that time she had given no hint, at least not to me, of an inclination to begin a career as an author. So, when she brought a copy of *Exit* to my office for me to read, I was, to put it mildly, surprised. I was also grateful that she bought it to me on a Friday afternoon, because I could not put the book down, except for the most necessary of personal activities, until I was finished. Frankie can sure tell a story!

But another word was lurking in my subconscious mind, which did not surface until, one year later, when she brought me a copy of her second book, *Breaking the Chain*, to read. Once again I was drawn into the story, marveling at her artistic ability, when I suddenly realized that I was ignoring the other ingredient that made her stories so appealing—their authenticity. Mrs. Wise's WORK is authentic because SHE is authentic. She draws on her own personal experiences while growing up in a small town in the Jim Crow South. She captures, not only the conditions and the flavor of the era, but also the psychological-emotional mindset of the people, black and white, imposed on them by conventions and traditions of those times. So faithful is the depiction of that era that I dare say *Breaking the Chain* should be categorized as a work of historical fiction.

Breaking the Chain is not only entertaining, it may be important. In 2015, Frankie published *Broken Promises*, a play adapted from *Breaking the Chain*. My sincere hope is to see *Broken Promises* played out, not only on a theatrical stage but also on a sound stage when some alert screenwriter collaborates with Mrs. Wise to write the screenplay, and some television or movie and film producer recognizes it as a story that should be told.

Frankie asked me to edit *Broken Promises* for her and I agreed. When she brought me my own signed, hardback copy of the play, she also brought me another copy of *Breaking the Chain* and asked me to edit it for the second edition of the book. I accepted the new challenge with pleasure. I'm grateful for the privilege of participating in the development of a talented author's career. Thank you, Frankie!

Dr N Jeff Carden III

Dr. N. Jeff Carden, III – Editor

PREFACE

I dedicate this fictional novel to my grandmother, Lula Mae Bell Johnson Rutledge, my mother, Doris Rutledge Parham, and my brothers, Ted Berry and Allen Rutledge.

I want to give a special acknowledgement to my aunts, Gladys "Jittel" Rutledge Hill, Martha Rutledge Brown, and Baby Ruth Rutledge, and my uncles, Harvey and Cleveland Rutledge.

I also dedicate this novel to the people of LaGrange, Carrollton, Hogansville, Newnan, Roopville, and Franklin, Georgia—where I was born and raised. I would also like to mention the people of Roanoke, Alabama.

Many of you have been an important part of my life and have aided in my decision to write this book. The characters in *Breaking the Chain* are largely based on these encounters, both good and bad.

As you read this book, you may just be reading about yourself!

Frankie Berry Wise
Breaking the Chain
Started 1997, **Completed** 2016

CHAPTER 1

It was a bone-chilling December night. Iris lay in bed clinging to her worn-woolen blanket to keep warm. The wind wailed as it blew through the cracks of the wood-framed shotgun house, as the last flames in the fireplace began to flicker out.

Iris' bedroom became colder, darker, and eerier. She was afraid. Her grandmother, Sarah, had told her too many scary ghost stories.

Her grandmother and aunt, Rose, were sleeping soundly in the other bed while Iris laid awake thinking about her mother, Lilly.

Iris and her mother usually slept together, but Lilly was away working as a live-in maid for a white family. For now, Iris slept alone.

Finally, the last of the embers in the fireplace turned to ashes. The tree limbs banged their fists against the frail windowpanes, causing Iris to feel even colder. She thought of one of Sarah's many stories and imagined that she could hear the cries of a deceased little girl roaming the hall looking for her mother. Iris' fears became unbearable.

"Aunt Rose," Iris whispered.

"What?" Rose answered.

"I'm scared. I hear that little dead girl walking in the hall."

"It's only the wind. Go to sleep!"

"Can I sleep with you and Mama?"

"It's not enough room for the three of us."

“Then sleep with me,” Iris begged.

“It’s too cold to change beds and your bed smells like pee.”

Rose’s voice helped to ease Iris’ fears. She was hoping that Rose would continue talking so she could fall asleep under her soft voice, but the conversation ceased and Iris was still awake. Soon Iris felt a cold wind against her back. Someone had raised her covers and she feared it was a ghost.

“It’s me,” Rose whispered. “We need a man living here to keep us safe and the logs burning in the fireplace.”

“Uncle Cleo is a man,” Iris said. “Why is he always gone?”

“He’s a trapper,” Rose answered. “He spends most of his days and nights sleeping on the banks of the Chattahoochee River, catching fish and trapping animals for their meat and hides.”

“Get Mama to make him stop,” Iris begged.

“He makes a lot of money off those hides and the meat helps to feed us,” Rose said, continuing to whisper. “Let’s be quiet before we wake up Mama.”

“Too late,” Sarah said.

“Sorry Mama,” Rose said apologetically.

“Except for my son, Cleo,” Sarah said with an angry tone, “I don’t want to hear about another man living in this house.”

“Your daddy used to live with us and he left a bad taste in Mama’s mouth,” Rose whispered to Iris.

“I don’t have a daddy,” Iris responded.

“Everybody has a daddy, silly,” Rose said, softly giggling. “Your daddy's name is George Dawson."

"But if he is my daddy, where is he?" Iris asked.

"I'll tell you tomorrow," Rose said.

"You promise?" Iris asked.

"I promise," Rose replied.

Iris felt safe lying next to Rose. She could feel and smell Rose's warm breath against her neck.

Suddenly, Iris' eyelids became heavy. The sandman was on his way. It would soon be morning and she would remind Rose of her promise.

Iris closed her eyes and whispered, "God bless my grand-mama Sarah, my mama Lilly, my aunt Rose, and my uncle Cleo."

Rose then whispered for her to go to sleep. Iris drifted off to sleep underneath the blanket with Rose close beside her.

"Good night.

Sleep tight.

Don't let the bedbugs bite.

Soon it will be light.

They only come out at night."

CHAPTER 2

Iris awoke to the aroma of freshly brewed coffee and baked sweet potatoes. Sarah had already made her bed and had left for her job at Mr. Parker James' grocery store. Mr. Parker James lived in a small room in the back of his store.

Iris glanced at the logs burning in the fireplace. Rose was sitting in Sarah's rocking chair in front of the fireplace wearing a long white cotton nightgown. She was sipping hot coffee from a small china cup.

Iris jumped out of bed and ran into the cold kitchen. She pulled up her long nightgown around her waist and urinated into a chamber pot. She then hurried back into the bedroom before sitting on the floor in front of Rose and the fireplace. Iris noticed a large brown paper bag next to the rocking chair.

"It's for you," Rose said while handing it to her. "Lilly sent it by some woman who shops at Mr. James' store."

Iris opened the bag and found a blue and a green dress, four pairs of white socks, and two pairs of underwear. It all looked second-hand. There was also a small white doll dressed in a green corduroy dress. Iris named the blonde-haired, blue-eyed, doll Miss Ann.

"Why are the white dolls pretty and the black dolls ugly?" Rose asked, watching Iris playing with the doll.

"Are you white?" Iris asked.

"Why do you ask me that?" Rose questioned.

"Because you're pretty," Iris said, causing Rose to smile. "Is Mama, Uncle Cleo, and me white?"

"Almost," Rose answered. "That's why the colored folks don't like us and most of the white folks don't either, especially the white women. They know their men been messing in the black wash pot. We're just caught in the middle. Sometimes you can use it to your advantage. As you get older, you'll see what I mean."

"Tell me how I got a daddy," Iris begged.

"Promise me," Rose said sternly, "you won't tell Lilly or Cleo, and especially Mama."

"Cross my heart and hope to die," Iris promised.

"Well," Rose began as she settled into the rocking chair, "one day George Dawson, the man who would become your daddy, just showed up at Mr. James' store. That's where your grandmother first met your daddy. He came all the way from Texas looking for Mr. James. He was a good-looking man, about six feet tall, and weighed around two hundred and fifty pounds. He looked white, but Mama said he was colored. Mr. James insisted that George live with us for a few weeks, but it turned into months. Mama let George sleep on the twin bed in the backroom. After he moved in with us, George and Mama began to spend a lot of time together." Rose then chuckled before saying, "Mama was always going into his room and closing the door, but she forgot the doorknob was missing. I would peep inside the room and see what was going on."

"When Mama was at work," Rose continued, "Cleo, Lilly, and me were left at the house in George's care. Just as soon as he was sure Mama was gone, George would tell Cleo to take Mama's rifle and go shoot some squirrels for our supper. He'd tell me to play under the house and fool the doodlebugs out of their holes. George said Lilly had to wash the dirty breakfast dishes. I never believed him because Mama always washed the dishes before she went to work. When Cleo and me were out of the house, George would take Lilly into his room and close the door. I began to wonder if George and Lilly were doing the same thing as him and Mama did."

She paused before continuing, "Lilly was not allowed to talk to the town's colored boys. When a boy would attempt to visit the house to court Lilly, Mama would tell him to scat. She didn't want her daughter being courted by them colored boys and maybe getting pregnant and having a dark-skinned baby. Mama told George, when she was not home, to keep a lookout for boys coming by to see Lilly and to chase them away. It was a job he gladly accepted."

Iris listened as Rose continued. "So one day, I decided to slip back into the house early. I could already hear the bedsprings on George's bed screeching and him moaning. It was the same sounds that I used to hear when he and Mama were in the bedroom. I peeped through the missing doorknob hole. Sure enough, I saw George naked and on top of Lilly. He was moving up and down on top of her just like he did on Mama. George was so much bigger than Lilly that I could barely see her small body. I hurried back outdoors so George would think his secret was safe with him and Lilly. I would put a small twig into a doodlebug's hole." Rose then leaned back in her chair, closed her eyes, and softly began to sing.

"Doodlebug, Doodlebug, won't you come out to play?

Come out to play; Come out to play with me today."

The fire in the fireplace had begun to fizzle out. Cold air seeped through the planks of the floor and under the kitchen door, chilling the room. Rose stopped singing her doodlebug song. She opened her eyes and looked into the fireplace and noticed that the logs had almost burned away.

"George kept messing around with Mama and Lilly until Mama noticed that Lilly's stomach was beginning to swell and she was queasy all the time," Rose said. "One day, Mama told me and Cleo to sit with her in the swing. She sat between us and asked if we had seen any boys slipping around the house to see Lilly while she was at work. We told her the truth and said, 'No, ma'am.' So Mama told us to stay where we were and went into the house to talk to Lilly. We could hear Mama and Lilly talking through the window. She asked her, 'Have you let a boy get between your legs?' Lilly then began to cry and quickly confessed that it was George. Mama and the sheriff looked for George all that day, but could not find him. Mama took a warrant out for his arrest for messing with a child. George hid for a week before they discovered he had been at Mrs. Cora Mae Butler's house that whole time. By the time they realized this, he had already skipped town on a train. He left your mama to take the blame for her pregnancy all by herself."

The look on Rose's face showed the pain of reliving the memories that she was now talking about. Although Iris was hearing about the story of her mother and father for the first time, she was no less consciously, or unconsciously, pained by it.

Rose continued, "Lilly's stomach grew so big. The last month she had to stay, eat, and use the bedpan in bed with her back propped up on pillows. Mama feared that she would die giving birth. Mrs. Cora Mae Butler was the midwife, who usually delivered all the colored babies in Crosstown. But, Mama wanted Lilly to have a real doctor. Besides, she hated Mrs. Cora Mae for hiding George until he could sneak away. Mr. James said that he would get his good white friend, Dr. Peter O' Casey, to deliver you. Mr. James came by the house just about every day to check on Lilly and bring her a Baby Ruth candy bar or some cookies from his store. Many days, Mr. James told Mama not to come to work so she could stay home and care for your mama. You would have thought Lilly was having Mr. James' grandchild. It's rumored that Mr. James is my, Cleo's, and your Uncle John's daddy because we could all pass for white, except for Lilly. Even though Lilly is very light, if you look closely, you can tell her daddy may have been a darker-skinned man."

Rose stood up from sitting in Sarah's rocking chair and said, "Dr. O' Casey was a redheaded Irishman, who loved whiskey and good southern cooking. He was the town drunk. His whole body smelled of moonshine. He agreed to be Lilly's doctor if Mama kept a lot of moonshine for him to drink and home-cooked food for him to eat. Since Mama agreed to his demands, Dr. O' Casey didn't mind sleeping on a cot in the same bedroom with us colored women while we gossiped about the crackers in Crosstown, Georgia."

Iris listened more attentively than ever. Rose said, "Early one morning, Lilly began to have a very bad stomach ache. She began to cry as she twisted and turned in her bed. She begged Mama to make the pain stop. Mama told her that the baby was coming. Dr. O' Casey stumbled off his cot and examined Lilly. She cried for hours until finally it was time for her to push you out. It was not a pretty sight. Thank goodness Mama sent your uncle, Cleo, to hunt in the backwoods until dark. Cleo didn't know much about girls getting pregnant and having babies. I think he still believed a stork delivered babies to people's houses. Seeing you popping out of Lilly would have scared him to death. Mama could not take the chance of Cleo, her only son after your uncle, John, was killed in the war, running into the woods and never returning. When Cleo got home, you were already here and sound asleep in the bed with Lilly."

Rose sighed before finishing, "Lilly screamed as she pushed you out, 'Mama it hurts!' I helped to hold her legs wide open while Dr. O' Casey pulled on your head. 'Grunt down like you do when you are constipated,' Mama said until you finally popped out. You were born on a cold day in February. And that is how you got a daddy."

Feeling like there was more to explain, Rose said, "Soon after you were born, Lilly had to find a job. She worked as a live-in maid, leaving me to care for you while she took care of someone else's white children."

Rose stared into the fire for a long time before going into the kitchen to get more logs for the fireplace. Iris got up off the floor and sat in Sarah's rocking chair and rocked back and forth while holding her new doll, Miss Ann. She and Rose could only sit in the rocking chair when Sarah was at work. When Sarah was home, the chair belonged to her.

As Iris watched Rose add more firewood, Miss Ann suddenly cried out, "M-m-mama." Iris was shocked that Miss Ann could talk. She was a special doll and Iris vowed to keep her forever.

She continued to rock Miss Ann while Rose laid down for a nap. Rose quickly fell asleep and began to snore. Iris stomach growled from hunger pangs, but the last sweet potato belonged to Sarah. For now, Iris would have to wait until Sarah came home with their supper.

* * * * *

The sound of Sarah's footsteps moved heavily across the loosened planks of the porch. Iris laid Miss Ann on the floor and hurried to open the door for Sarah. With her long salt and pepper hair, pale skin, and reddish nose—Sarah rushed past Iris carrying their supper on a platter that was covered with a dishtowel. As Sarah went into the kitchen, Iris inhaled the aroma of fried chicken, string beans, and corn muffins.

"Rose!" Sarah yelled as she divided up the food. "After you eat, I need you to help me spruce up the bedroom across the hall. The town is building a new school for white children!"

"What's that got to do with us?" Rose asked as she crawled out of bed.

"Boarders! That's what it got to do with us," Sarah said, bringing the food into the bedroom. She gave Rose and Iris their plates and sat in her rocking chair. "Mayor Berry came in the store today. He said that he was trying to think of a good colored family to board three colored men for the next six months. The men are coming to build the new schoolhouse. He asked Mr. James if they could stay with me and he said that he didn't mind. Besides, we sure could use the extra money. They should be here sometime this week."

Sarah glanced at Miss Ann and asked, "Where did that white doll come from?"

"She was at the bottom of that bag of clothes that Lilly sent," Rose answered.

Iris picked up the doll and proudly said, “I named her Miss Ann.”

“That’s a good name for a white doll,” Sarah said as she handed them a fruit jar filled with water from which they all took turns drinking.

CHAPTER 3

Three colored men came to live in Sarah's house as boarders while they worked on building the new schoolhouse.

It was taking longer to build it than expected; six months turned into a year and a year turned into two years. One worker would quit and Mayor Berry would have to hire another one to take his place. So many different colored men came and went from Sarah's house that Iris could not remember all of their names. But, she would always remember the boarder named Mr. Joe Fish. Among all the boarders, he lived with them the longest.

On the weekends, all the workers went home to visit their families—except Mr. Fish. He did not have any immediate family, so he usually hung around the house. Sarah and Mr. Fish would sit on the porch talking for hours, long after Iris and Rose had gone to bed.

With the extra money they got from the boarders, Sarah and Lilly had saved enough for Iris to attend Mrs. Cora Mae Butler's Finishing School for Colored Girls so she could go to college at the famous Tuskegee Institute in Tuskegee, Alabama.

Although Sarah hated Mrs. Cora Mae, she knew that her school was the only place Iris could get an education. It was rumored that Lilly's rapist and Iris' father, George Dawson, also dated Mrs. Cora Mae. When he was a fugitive for molesting Lilly, he promised Mrs. Cora Mae that he would send for her later if she hid him from the law until he could flee Crosstown, Georgia.

None of that mattered to Sarah anymore. She had once sought a better life for all of her children. However, she was now devoting all of her energy and limited resources to ensuring her granddaughter, Iris, could become a teacher.

Her first child, John, had fought and died during the war in Germany. He joined the army when he was only sixteen years old. Sarah begged him not to join, but he insisted. He did not want to be a hunter and fisherman like his younger brother, Cleo, was destined to be, nor a farmer like most of the colored men in Crosstown.

John was highly intelligent. He decided to join the military in hopes of becoming a colonel because he wanted to make Sarah proud.

In one of his letters that he wrote home to Sarah, he described the horrors of war. He always ended his letters by promising to return home safely and by telling Sarah to think of him whenever she heard the sounds of a plane flying across the sky.

Six months after John left for Germany, Sarah was busy working in Mr. Parker James' store. It was the first Saturday in June when most people, white and colored, did their monthly shopping. Everyone in the store suddenly stopped, what he or she was doing, when two uniformed soldiers walked inside.

Only Sarah and a white family, Mr. and Mrs. Ned Lambert, had sons serving in the war. The Lambert family had already received the news of their son's death two months prior.

On this day, everyone knew it must be Sarah who was going to receive the devastating news.

The soldiers, one colored and one white, entered Mr. James' store. It was the first time a colored person had entered, besides Sarah, using the front door. The sign over the door read, "Whites only." If colored folks wanted to shop, they had to enter and exit through the back door.

The colored soldier was the first to speak. He said, "We asked someone in town where we could find Miss Sarah Jackson's house. We were told that we could find her working at this store."

All of the customers pointed toward Sarah. She instinctively knew if soldiers were looking for her, it had to be about her son, John, and that it must be bad news.

As the two soldiers slowly approached her, Sarah's heart began to beat faster and faster. She prayed that John was just wounded and that he would soon be on his way back home. But, her prayers would not be answered on that first Saturday in June. The news was much worse.

The white soldier, holding papers in his hand, stood motionless with an austere look on his face. However, the colored soldier seemed more sympathetic. He walked a little closer to Sarah and said, "Miss Jackson, we are sorry to inform you that your son, John Jackson, has been killed on the battlefield and his body is being shipped home for burial."

The white soldier then handed Sarah the papers he was holding and said, "The U.S. Army sends you condolences."

Upon hearing the news of her son's death, Sarah dropped the papers on the floor and ran out of the back door screaming, "Why, God? Why?"

As she stood, alone and sobbing in the parking lot, she suddenly heard the sound of an airplane passing overhead. She looked up and saw the airplane moving slowly across the clear blue sky.

On the sleeve of her dress, she wiped the tears from her eyes as she watched the airplane until it was out of sight. Sarah envisioned that John was sitting inside, waving goodbye through one of its small windows.

Finally, Mr. Parker James came out of his store and told Sarah to go home so she could be with her family. He then closed his store early that Saturday in June to secretly mourn John's death. Mr. James kept his grieving for John a secret just as he had kept the fact that he had fathered him.

John was given a military funeral. The American flag that draped his casket was carefully folded by the servicemen and given to Sarah.

Mr. James sat next to her as his casket was lowered into its final resting place.

John's death was especially heart wrenching for his brother, Cleo. They were very close; John loved his brother. He was the only person who understood Cleo's unorthodox behavior.

After John's death, Cleo became more reclusive. He lived most of his days and nights in the woods trapping, hunting, fishing, and roaming the banks of the Chattahoochee River.

He slept in a sleeping bag, under the summer skies, until Mr. James gifted him with a tent. Later, he built himself a shack in the woods. Cleo survived by cooking his food on a campfire. His cuisine consisted of mostly wild roots, leafy greens, and game that he caught.

Cleo would only come home long enough to bring freshly killed meat and catfish to Sarah. He would come up the road pulling a makeshift sled loaded with animal pelts and furs for Rose to pack and ship to the Fur and Leather Company in Chicago.

Cleo always shared his earnings with Sarah. She would save the money so she could one day move out of the house that Mr. James owned, buy her own home, and pay for Iris to attend college.

On the other hand, Rose found enjoyment in lying around the house, babysitting Iris, and reading Sarah's romance novels. Rose's laziness and lack of interest in boys was perfectly fine with Sarah. She believed that even though Rose would probably not amount to much in life, her beauty would allow her to marry a rich man.

As for Lilly, Sarah believed that she would never amount to anything more than being a maid. She once had faith that Lilly would also go to college. But, after becoming a young mother, those aspirations had long subsided.

For now, Sarah considered Iris her last and final hope of seeing one of the Jackson's attend college.

CHAPTER 4

One blistering hot Sunday afternoon in August, Rose and Iris were sitting on the front porch. Iris was holding Miss Ann in her lap while Rose was reading aloud from one of Sarah's books until the mosquitoes and gnats became too unbearable for her flawless skin.

"It's hot out here!" Rose cried, slapping away insects with her hand. "Let's go inside!"

"I don't want to," Iris replied, reaching for the book in Rose's hand. "I want to stay out here and read to Miss Ann. I'm going to wait on Mama to get home."

"Enjoy that doll," Rose said, giving the book to Iris. "Soon you'll have to put her away."

"Why will I have to put her away?" Iris asked, holding tightly to Miss Ann.

"She's not a real person," Rose said to the defiant Iris. "You can put Miss Ann away for the real baby you'll have someday."

"I don't want a real baby! I'm happy with Miss Ann," Iris retorted.

Rose then went into the house to take a nap and left Iris on the porch. Iris stared at Rose through the bedroom window. Even on the hottest of days, Rose would pull the bedcovers over her head to keep the mosquitoes from biting her.

Iris continued to read aloud to Miss Ann when Mr. Joe Fish walked onto the porch.

"What are you doing?" Mr. Fish asked. "Reading to your pretty doll?"

Iris recognized Mr. Fish by his strong odor, even before she looked up from her book. His breath and body reeked of sardines and whiskey.

On the first of the month, after collecting her rent, Sarah was going to tell Mr. Fish that he had to find another place to live. She was growing tired of him consuming liquor in her house. She was also fed up with the unsavory glances he would give Rose and Iris when he was intoxicated.

"Yes, sir," Iris answered, not taking her eyes off her book. She wondered if he was called Mr. Fish because he ate so many sardines.

"Does your doll have a name?"

"Miss Ann."

"That's a good name for a white doll."

"Thank you."

"Do you want to go in the house with me? I got some pennies for you in my room, but we got to be very quiet. We can't let your aunt, Rose, know. She may get jealous and want some of your pennies for herself."

The other boarders would sometimes give Iris and Rose pennies to buy candy from Mr. James' store. The thought of extra pennies to buy more candy was enticing to Iris.

She left Miss Ann and her book laying in the swing and followed Mr. Fish into the house.

Mr. Fish held Iris' hand as they quietly walked down the hallway and went into his room. Once inside, he closed his door. He then picked Iris up and sat her on his bed. He removed a bottle of homemade wine from his back pocket, opened it, and handed it to her.

"Try some," he said, persuading her.

Iris took the bottle of wine from Mr. Fish and began to drink it. She thought it tasted just like a grape soda.

Mr. Fish set the bottle on top of his nightstand before pushing Iris down on the bed. Her head rested on his pillow, which reeked of sardine oil. Iris began to feel dizzy. She tried to push him away, but Mr. Fish held her down with his entire body. When she tried to cry out for Rose, he placed one hand over her mouth and whispered, "If you don't stay still and be quiet, I'll burn this raggedy house down while you and Rose and Sarah are sleeping."

He then lifted her blue dress above her head, pulled down her panties, and spread her legs far apart. He began to rub his penis against her vagina.

Iris was petrified as she lay on his bed with her dress covering her face. She suddenly remembered the story that Rose had told her about her mother, Lilly, and what her father, George Dawson, had done to her. Ironically, she now lay naked in the same room and on the same bed.

Iris silently wept at the thought that she too would become a young mother and give birth with the help of a drunken Dr. O' Casey.

Abruptly, Mr. Fish jumped off of Iris. He pulled her panties back up around her waist and her dress down from her face. Disgusted with himself and realizing the crime that he had just committed—he quickly lifted Iris off his bed, opened his door, and shoved her into the hallway.

Iris stood in the hallway and watched Mr. Fish remove the pillowcase off of his pillow and fill it with the few belongings he owned. He threw the pillowcase over his shoulder and rushed past Iris, almost knocking her to the floor. Without saying a word, he dashed out of the back door never to be seen or heard from again.

Iris went back to where she had left her doll. She took Miss Ann in the house and went into her room, where Rose was still asleep.

Iris' thoughts swirled around her in desperate confusion. She wondered, "Is Aunt Rose pretending to be asleep? Did she see what happened between Mr. Fish and me? Is she going to tell my grandmother?"

Iris took off her fishy smelling clothes. She surmised that Sarah would surely be able to smell Mr. Fish's odor on her. Iris had often smelled the same odor on her grandmother, Sarah, when she would vanish into Mr. Fish's bedroom late at night. Had Sarah been secretly sleeping with Mr. Fish?

Iris took a clean pair of panties and a wrinkled green dress from her dresser drawer. She carried Miss Ann and the outfit into the kitchen where she changed her clothes. She then stuffed her dirty blue dress and panties deep into a hole, inside the wall, behind the kitchen stove. Although her blue dress was one of her favorites, seeing it again would only remind Iris of the horrible encounter with Mr. Joe Fish. As she pushed her fishy smelling clothes deeper into the hole, using the handle of a broom, she remembered the conversation she had with Rose earlier that day. Rose told her that one of these days that she would have to put Miss Ann away and have a real baby.

Believing that she would soon bear Mr. Fish's child and Sarah would hate her like she hated Lilly—Iris took Miss Ann off the kitchen table and also stuffed her into the same hole. She surmised that the rats would probably eat them before anyone would discover them. Before forcing the last of her doll's legs into the hole, Iris tearfully said, "I'll never forget you Miss Ann."

Iris returned to the porch, sat in the swing, and waited for Sarah to come home.

Soon afterwards, Rose jumped out of bed and hurried to the porch. She sat next to Iris. Rose was panicking, yet relieved to find that Sarah was not home because she was not supposed to leave Iris unsupervised.

"Sorry Iris for leaving you all by yourself for so long," Rose explained.

“That’s okay,” Iris responded, beginning to cry.

“Why are you crying?”

“Because Mr. Fish carried me into his room and...”

“What did he do to you?” Rose interrupted.

“Nothing,” Iris said, embarrassed.

“Please don’t tell Mama that I left you alone on the porch and that you were in Mr. Fish’s room. He’ll be gone on the first of the month, anyway. You won’t ever have to see him again.” Rose reiterated, “Do you promise not to tell?”

“I promise!”

“Good girl… because Mama would kill me if she knew! Now dry your eyes. Here comes Mama now.”

Sarah walked onto the porch and sat between them. In an angry tone, she said, “My friend Wade just left Mr. James’ store buying his groceries! He said that he saw Joe Fish by the train station waiting to steal a ride on a boxcar! He said that Joe had a pillowcase thrown over his shoulder! I bet that son-of-bitch stole my pillowcase to use for a suitcase and skipped town without paying me my damn money!” Sarah looked directly at Iris and asked, “Did you see or speak to Mr. Fish today?”

“No, ma’am,” Iris cried. She jumped up from the swing and immediately ran into the house with Sarah following quickly after her.

Rose reluctantly followed behind them. She went into Mr. Fish’s room to search for any clues that he might have left behind.

Iris got in her bed and hid her face under the covers.

“What’s wrong with you, Iris?” Sarah asked, sitting on the edge of her bed. “Are you worried about starting school tomorrow?”

“Yes, ma’am,” Iris said, with her eyes tightly closed. She regretted that she was lying to Sarah. She wanted to tell Sarah the truth about what Mr. Fish had done to her, but she had promised Rose that she would not.

“If you’re worried about how Mrs. Cora Mae will be paid, Lilly and I have saved enough money. I have a surprise for you, too. Those white folks let Lilly have tomorrow off from work. She’ll be home early in the morning to be with you on your first day of school. Do you feel better now?”

Iris began to cry even harder.

“Is there something else bothering you?” Sarah asked.

“Rose said one day, I’ll have a real baby,” Iris cried. “If I have a real baby, I can’t go to school.”

“My sweet child,” Sarah said, “you won’t have a baby until you start getting your period once a month like Rose and Lilly. Once you finish Mrs. Cora Mae’s school—you’ll go to college in Alabama, get married, and then have a baby. Rose was only teasing you.”

“I’m not going to have a baby?” Iris asked, remembering that there was never blood in her panties.

“Not until your period starts. But when it does, don’t let a boy get between your legs. You hear me?” Sarah demanded.

“Yes, ma’am,” Iris replied, feeling better and hoping Mr. Fish was gone for good. She did not want Sarah to ever know what happened in his room. Like her aunt, Rose, she would continue to be Sarah’s sweet little girl.

Sarah held Iris’ hand and said, “Let’s go in Fish’s room and see if

Rose found anything."

"I don't want to go in his room," Iris cried while clinging to her bed covers. "You said there were ghosts in that room!"

"Fear only the living," Sarah said. "Now come on!"

"Mama," Rose said from the hallway, "Mr. Fish's things are gone."

"Are you sure?" Sarah asked, not particularly surprised.

"Yes, ma'am," Rose answered. "His drawers and closet is empty."

You could see the fire in Sarah's eyes. She looked like she was judge, jury, and executioner. Iris wondered if Sarah's anger was because she secretly knew what Mr. Fish had done to her or was she angry at being abandoned by yet another man in her life?

Sarah's sharp words cut through the tense air, breaking Iris' thoughts and startling Rose. "May you burn in HELL, Joe Fish! You low-down, stinking, high-yellow, trashy, son-of-a-bitch!"

CHAPTER 5

Iris awoke the next morning to find Lilly standing at the foot of her bed. As promised, she was there to walk her to school for her first day.

Lilly was wearing a gray dress. Gray was always her favorite color. Iris thought her mother looked so young and beautiful. When she opened her eyes, Lilly smiled at her. Seeing the smile on her mother's face helped to ease some of the horror that Iris had just endured the day before with Mr. Joe Fish.

Iris got out of bed and anxiously looked into the bag that Lilly had for her. Inside it was a new white ruffled blouse, a plaid skirt, and a pair of black baby doll shoes. Lilly had recently purchased them from a local department store using the money she received from her job as a maid. The department store allowed her to pay a little towards them each week. After three months, she had finally saved enough to pay the remaining balance.

Iris felt like a little princess in her new clothes. Lilly helped her comb her long, black hair into a ponytail. Her hair was so long that it was hanging down her back. Iris was finally ready to attend the only school in Crosstown, Georgia for colored girls to get an education.

Because Mrs. Cora Mae thought that colored girls were deprived, she founded a finishing school for them so that they could have a better future in lieu of marrying early, having children, working as a maid, or breaking their backs picking cotton for the white man. She originally financed her school with the money she earned selling catfish on the weekends. To keep it open, she would have to depend on the small amount of fees she charged parents to teach their children.

Iris was very lucky to be one of the twelve girls chosen to attend her school, especially since Mrs. Cora Mae and her grandmother,

Sarah, hated each other. Mrs. Cora Mae despised Sarah because she believed that she had had an affair with her husband, Benny, which ultimately gave him the courage to leave her. Sarah hated her for similar reasons. She blamed Mrs. Cora Mae for helping George Dawson escape justice.

Nevertheless, they put their differences aside. Both of them could now benefit from the other and this time, no man would stand in their way. Sarah wanted Iris to ultimately go to college and had the money to pay her tuition, in full, and Mrs. Cora Mae needed the extra money and refused to take out her hatred on the innocent Iris.

Lilly and Iris walked down the rocky dirt road towards Mrs. Cora Mae's school. Lilly held Iris' hand as if she were more of an older sister protecting her younger sister than as a mother with her child.

Lilly was elated to have those few moments alone with her daughter. It was not Lilly's choice to leave Iris at home to be raised by Sarah and Rose while she worked out of town for a rich white family. But, she needed the money to help Sarah pay bills and to save for Iris' private education. Lilly wanted Iris to have a better life than she, Rose, or Sarah had ever had.

As the school came into their sight, Iris tightly gripped Lilly's hand. Lilly only had a few more minutes to break the silence and have a conversation with the daughter that she hardly ever got an opportunity to see.

"We're almost there," Lilly said. "Don't be afraid. You'll make lots of new friends."

"I want to go back home!" Iris begged.

"You can't. I promise this is the right choice for you… you'll see."

"Are you going to stay with me?"

"As long as I can, but I have to go back to work."

"When are you coming home to stay?"

"Soon… but, in the meantime be a good girl. I want you to listen and learn from Mrs. Cora Mae. And don't forget to obey your grandmother! If you look around and don't see me, I'll be gone back to work. Your aunt, Rose, will be here when school gets out to walk you back home." Lilly hesitated before saying, "Remember, Iris, that I love you."

"I love you, too," Iris said with a fearful expression on her face.

When Iris and Lilly entered the one-room schoolhouse, Mrs. Cora Mae stood up from her desk and introduced the students to them.

"Girls," Mrs. Cora Mae said, "this is Iris and her mother, Miss Lilly. Iris will be a new student at our school. Say hello to Miss Lilly and welcome Iris to the class."

"Hello, Miss Lilly. Welcome to our class, Iris," the girls said in unison as they sat at their desks.

After Lilly was introduced to the class, Mrs. Cora Mae suggested that it would be best for Iris if Lilly left. Lilly smiled at her daughter and complied with Mrs. Cora Mae's request. Iris wanted to cry, but she knew the other girls would laugh and tease her.

After Lilly left, Mrs. Cora Mae let the girls mingle. The students were of various ages so it was hard for Iris to figure out where she fit in. Eventually, the girls congregated in a huddle and began to whisper to each other. Only Iris and Mrs. Cora Mae's granddaughter, Annie, were excluded.

After several weeks had passed, it became apparent that Iris and Annie were not going to fit in with the other girls. Sarah said that it was because Iris was too pretty and white and Annie was too black and boyish. Annie was the only one out of the twelve girls who wore pants to school. The Jones twins, Mattie and Hattie, always made fun of her. At recess, they would sing:

"Annie is a boy. Annie is a boy.

How do we know?

Because our mama said so.

Annie is a boy. Annie is a boy.

My mama ought to know.

When Annie was on her way,

My mama helped that day.

Annie is a boy. Annie is a boy.

This we know!"

Iris and Annie, the two outcasts of the class, became best friends. They sat next to each other in class, shared their lunch, and played together during recess. It was the first time that Iris had ever been around anyone with skin as dark as Annie's or a girl who wore pants. The females Iris had been around did not wear pants even when they picked cotton in the fields.

When Mrs. Cora Mae insisted that Annie had to wear a dress to Parent's Day, she looked so uncomfortable and sad that she sat in a corner and cried most of that day. It was the last time Iris would see Annie in a dress.

After months of being best friends, Sarah allowed Iris to sleep over at Annie's house. Sarah was against Iris staying overnight at Mrs. Cora Mae's, but Iris begged and pleaded until Sarah finally agreed.

After school, the following week, Iris went home with Annie. As they caught fireflies and put them in a jar, they talked about their future dreams and plans after graduation.

"I want to make my family proud," Iris said. "I want to attend the famous Tuskegee Institute in Alabama and become a teacher. I also want to establish my own school in Crosstown like your grandmother did. But, my school would be for colored boys, too. Someday, I want to marry a rich man and have a baby boy or a baby girl… What do you want to do, Annie?"

"If I could leave Crosstown today, I would move to Detroit. I hate this town and its people."

"Why?"

"They call me a freak because there's something different about me."

"What's different about you?"

"If I told you, you wouldn't understand. If you knew, you wouldn't be my friend either."

"I'd always be your friend, Annie. If you move to Detroit, where would you live and what would you do?"

"I'd live with Aunt Evelyn until I get a job in one of those factories. She works in one and makes a lot of money," Annie said proudly. "Then I'd get my own apartment and never return to Crosstown or down south again."

Iris and Annie ended their conversation when Mrs. Cora Mae summoned them inside to eat supper. After eating, they washed the dishes before doing their homework by an oil lamp.

Once their homework was completed, Mrs. Cora Mae held the lamp for them until they changed into their nightgowns. They then got into Annie's bed and covered themselves with one of Mrs. Cora Mae's handmade quilts.

"You girls go to sleep. Tomorrow is a school day and I don't want to hear a lot of talking and giggling."

"Yes, ma'am," Annie answered.

"That goes for you too, Iris."

"Yes, ma'am," Iris responded.

"Goodnight girls," Mrs. Cora Mae said as she left the bedroom.

Mrs. Cora Mae carried the oil lamp down the hallways to her bedroom, leaving Annie's room dark. The only flicker of light came from the fireflies that Annie and Iris had caught earlier and released into the room. The only sound in the room was the noise of a cricket until Annie whispered into Iris' ear, "Want to play a game?"

"What kind of game?" Iris asked, a little too loudly.

"Quiet," Annie whispered. "We don't want Grandmama to hear us."

Annie pulled the quilt over her and Iris' heads. She took Iris' hand and placed it on her protruding vagina and she placed her hand on Iris'.

"Play with mine and I'll play with yours while I stick my tongue in your mouth," Annie said.

"I don't want to play this game," Iris protested. "Who taught you this game, anyway?"

"My aunt's friend, Miss Joanne. We played this game when she lived with my grandmother. We stopped once she moved to Mississippi. At first, I hated this game, but I learned to like it. You will too."

"No, I won't! I don't want to play this game, Annie," Iris whispered, remembering what Mr. Joe Fish had done to her.

"Don't you want to be my best friend?" Annie asked.

"Yes," Iris said reluctantly.

"Promise me you'll always keep our secret," Annie demanded.

"I promise. We're best friends," Iris whispered, as she and Annie continued their game until they drifted off to sleep.

* * * * *

Iris awoke the next morning alone in the bedroom. The door was ajar, allowing her to hear Annie, in the kitchen, talking to Mrs. Cora Mae. Iris sat on the edge of the bed and listened.

She heard Annie sobbing while lying to her grandmother. Annie was telling Mrs. Cora Mae about the game they were playing the night before. She claimed that it was Iris who initiated it. Iris could not believe that Annie would tell their secret. Furthermore, she was flabbergasted that Annie would outright lie about it being her idea.

"Don't you worry baby," Mrs. Cora Mae said. "I'll protect you from that little slut. Shame on Iris! I ought to tell Sarah, but she's a slut, too. She's the reason your granddaddy left me!"

"I don't want to ever see Iris again," Annie sobbed. "Can I go and live with Aunt Evelyn? Since she owns a house and a beauty parlor, she can teach me how to be a beautician. Aunt Evelyn said that I was always welcome to live with her. Can I move to Detroit and live with her, please?"

"Are you sure that's what you want to do?"

"Yes, ma'am."

"I'll see if I can get you on a train tomorrow," Mrs. Cora Mae said, nodding in agreement.

"Thank you, Grandmama," Annie whimpered.

"Go to my room, Annie!" Mrs. Cora Mae demanded. "Don't come out until I come and get you! I want to give Iris her breakfast and have a little talk with her."

"Yes, ma'am," Annie said as she left the kitchen.

Iris could hear Annie walking down the hallway. Annie stopped briefly in front of her bedroom door before continuing on to Mrs. Cora Mae's room and closing the door behind her.

"Iris!" Mrs. Cora Mae yelled. "Come and eat your breakfast!"

"I'm not hungry," Iris yelled back. "Can I just get dressed for school?"

"Not until you eat your breakfast," Mrs. Cora Mae said sternly.

Iris got out of bed and came into the kitchen. She sat at the table, trying to avoid making eye contact with Mrs. Cora Mae. Iris could feel her anger from across the table.

Mrs. Cora Mae set Iris' plate—filled with grits overflowing with butter, two runny eggs, and a greasy sausage—on the table. She then sat down beside her.

"Iris, eat your breakfast," Mrs. Cora Mae said, giving a tug at her nightgown.

"I'm not hungry!" Iris protested, staring at the plate of slop.

"I guess you're too full off of sin," Mrs. Cora Mae said sarcastically. "The Bible says people like you are not welcome in Heaven, but I'm going to pray for you. If you repent, God might forgive you."

"Will God forgive Annie for the lies she told on me this morning? Will God forgive you, Mrs. Cora Mae, for believing Annie's lies?"

"Don't sass me, young lady! Go get dressed so I can walk you home! I'm closing school for today."

Before returning to Annie's room, Iris went to Mrs. Cora Mae's bedroom door. She knocked, but Annie did not answer. If Annie was really leaving, Iris felt compelled to at least say goodbye. She wanted Annie to know that she forgave her for lying and that she still valued their friendship.

Iris slowly opened the bedroom door and walked in. Annie was still wearing her nightgown. She was standing tall and lean like a bronze statue as she stared out of the window. A light breeze blew the lace curtains against Annie's velvety face. Suddenly, Iris felt a deep attraction for her.

"Annie," Iris said, her voice quivering, "I wasn't going to tell anyone about what we did last night. I don't want you to go; I'll miss you. You are my one and only friend. If you leave, I'll be all alone!"

"Iris, I'm..."

"Annie, what are you trying to tell me?"

"I'm not like you. I'm different."

"How are you different?"

"I love you," Annie said, stuttering.

"I love you, too."

"My love is not the same as your love."

"Iris," Mrs. Cora Mae yelled from the kitchen. "Come out of my room and leave Annie alone! I told you to get dressed!"

"Goodbye Annie," Iris said, turning to leave. "I'm glad you got your wish to go to Detroit. Take care. I will always love you."

Iris walked out of Mrs. Cora Mae's room with her head bowed. She went back into Annie's bedroom and got dressed. She then sat on the edge of the bed, nervously waiting until Mrs. Cora Mae was ready to walk her home.

Iris and Mrs. Cora Mae walked side-by-side down the dirt road toward Iris' house. Mrs. Cora Mae told her to tell Sarah that she was closing the school, for the day, because she had some important business to take care of downtown. She asked Iris to keep what happened between her and Annie a secret.

As Iris approached her house, she could see Rose and the new boarder, Mr. Charlie Sweet, sitting on the porch. Mrs. Cora Mae watched from the distance as Iris walked the rest of the way home alone.

Iris walked past Rose and Mr. Charlie Sweet, pretending to smile. She was trying her best to mask the hidden sadness, betrayal, hurt, embarrassment, and guilt she was feeling.

For now, she would have to tuck what happened between her and Annie into the far corners of her mind—the way she had once tucked her doll, Miss Anne, and her fishy smelling clothes away in that hole behind the stove.

Iris wondered if she would ever see her best friend again. As she sat in Sarah's rocking chair, she whispered to herself, "Don't forget me Annie."

CHAPTER 6

Mr. Charlie Sweet was the first and the last white boarder to ever live in Sarah's home; all of her prior boarders were colored men. Because the building of the new school, which would be attended by only white children, was taking longer than anticipated, he was hired as the foreman in charge of overseeing the workers in hopes that he could speed up the progress.

Mr. Charlie Sweet used to live with a white family, but he preferred to hang around Sarah's house with the colored workers. The white residents in Crosstown had had enough of Mr. Charlie's "nigger-loving" ways, so he was not invited to live in their homes again.

When the schoolhouse was eventually completed, Mr. Charlie remained in Crosstown to help build an additional room onto the back of Mr. James' store. Since Mr. Charlie did not have a wife or children to return to like most of the other workers, he eagerly accepted the job.

Mr. James wanted the extra room built for Sarah, who had been sleeping in his room, on a cot, to care for him. After years of chain-smoking cigarettes, Mr. James had fallen ill with emphysema. He had become too sick to ride Sarah to and from work on one of his mules.

Mr. James informed Sarah that Mr. Charlie Sweet would continue to board with her while he built the extra room. She did not like it, but what could she say? Mr. James owned her house and was essentially her master.

Since Sarah had to care for Mr. James and also work in his store, Rose was left with the responsibilities of cooking for Iris and Mr. Charlie Sweet, cleaning the house, and washing clothes.

Rose would help Iris do her homework and ensure that she went to bed on time. She also kept Mr. Charlie Sweet's supper warm until he returned from work. To show his appreciation, Mr. Charlie would bring Rose a Baby Ruth candy bar from Mr. James' store or a freshly bloomed red rose from Sarah's garden.

Mr. Charlie Sweet gradually changed his bad habits. Instead of just bathing on Saturdays, he began to bathe almost every night in one of Sarah's washtubs. He kept his long, blonde hair shampooed and used a shoestring to tie it into a ponytail.

Iris noticed that Rose and Mr. Charlie were becoming fond of each other. When Sarah stayed away from home overnight to care for Mr. James, Mr. Charlie would often come home early from work to spend as much time with Rose as he could before returning the next morning.

A few times, Iris caught Rose and Mr. Charlie glancing romantically at each other. Iris knew that the last thing Sarah wanted was for Rose to become involved with a poor, moonshine drinking, white trash, man like Mr. Charlie Sweet.

Unbeknownst to them, Rose was building up the courage to tell Sarah that she and Mr. Charlie Sweet were in love, leaving Crosstown to get married, and that they would live in a town where she would not be recognized as colored. However, bad weather and an impending storm spoiled their plans.

It was a hot and dreary day. Dark clouds were roaming the southern skies. Bolts of lightning flashed, followed closely by booms of thunder. A terrible storm was headed to Crosstown, so Mrs. Cora Mae dismissed school earlier than usual and ordered the girls to hurry home.

Frightened and not stopping for a moment, Iris quickly ran home. She was surprised to find the house pitch black; it looked quieter than a graveyard. She walked slowly down the dark hallway, softly calling out to Rose without getting a response. Iris was hoping that she would find Rose in her bed, as usual, asleep. She then quietly opened her bedroom door and looked inside, but Rose was nowhere to be found.

Overcome with the fear of being alone in a house that was reputed to be haunted, Iris decided to flee back into the storm in an attempt to escape to Mrs. Cora Mae's house. But when she opened the front door, the strong winds were unbearable. Hail and rain started to dance on the tin roof. Iris felt trapped and unable to EXIT.

Suddenly, she heard laughter coming from Mr. Charlie Sweet's bedroom. His door was closed, but Iris could see light beaming through the hole of the missing doorknob. She peeped through the hole and saw Rose and Mr. Charlie Sweet lying nude on top of his bed. There were dimly lit candles that cast their shadows upon the wall. They were having sex.

Iris continued to watch them until a hand yanked her away by her long ponytail. Iris screamed because she thought it was a ghost, but it was Sarah. Iris would have preferred it be a ghost because Sarah's angry face made the storm seem tame.

Sarah flung Mr. Charlie Sweet's door wide open. She rushed in and grabbed him by his throat. She then pinned him against the wall with one hand and made a fist with her other. She began to punch him until his face was as red as a beet. Blood dripped from his nose.

"Please don't kill him, Mama!" Rose screamed. "I love Charlie!"

Sarah continued to punch Mr. Charlie Sweet anywhere her fist could land. Her punches echoed off of his skinny body. Rose tried to get dressed, but her trembling hands kept dropping her clothes. Finally, Rose found the courage to pull Sarah off and away from Mr. Charlie, allowing him to escape under the bed. Sarah then got down on her knees and glared at him.

"Come out from under this bed you white trash!" Sarah screamed.

"I'm sorry Miss Sarah… I didn't mean for you to find out about Rose and me this way," Mr. Charlie Sweet pleaded. "I love Rose. I'll never disappoint her. You got to believe me, Miss Sarah."

Sarah yelled angrily, "Now I know why I couldn't find you to help me lift Mr. James out of his bed! You were here cutting down my sweet daughter's cherry tree like you was George Washington with one of his slaves. Bring your sorry white ass from under this bed and face me like a man!"

"Don't come out, Charlie!" Rose yelled.

"Baby girl… my sweet Rose… how could you lay with that white trash, Charlie Sweet?" Sarah asked.

"We love each other, Mama," Rose said, her voice trembling. "We didn't mean for it to happen… it just did. Please Mama, you of all people should understand. I love Charlie the same way you love Mr. James. I'm going to have Charlie's baby and we're going to get married. Charlie will never deny me or his child the way Mr. James denied his love for you and us."

Iris was shocked to hear that Sarah and Mr. James were lovers and that he was the father of her mother, Lilly, aunt, Rose, and uncles, John and Cleo. Throughout the years, Iris had heard whispers and rumors amongst the black boarders such as, "Here comes Mr. G.W. for his cherry," when Mr. James would ride his mule to get Sarah for work. Iris wondered whether everyone, but her, knew about Mr. James and her grandmother.

When Sarah realized that Iris was standing in Mr. Charlie's doorway, with her mouth wide open and in shock at what she had just heard, she ordered her to leave the room. Iris immediately ran outside into the rain.

It seemed like Iris had been standing in the rain for an eternity when she finally decided to see what was happening in Mr. Charlie's room. She took a chair off the porch, set it under the window, stood in the chair, peered inside, and listened.

When she glanced through the windowpane, Iris saw Sarah lying on the floor like a snow angel. No longer nude, Mr. Charlie and Rose were standing over her. Iris wondered had they killed her grandmother until Sarah began to shout. She was too exhausted to stand, but not yet ready to give up the fight to save her beautiful daughter, Rose.

"I want you to leave my house, Charlie Sweet!" Sarah shouted, "Right now!"

"Yes, ma'am… but Rose is coming with me," Mr. Charlie Sweet replied, wiping the blood that dripped from his nose onto his handkerchief.

"No, she's not," Sarah snapped.

"Mama, my bag is already packed," Rose interjected. "I was going to tell you tomorrow, but I guess today is just as good." Rose grabbed a small leather suitcase that Sarah had given her on her eighteenth birthday. "When Charlie goes, I'm going with him."

"If you leave this house with that white trash," Sarah said, pointing her finger at Mr. Charlie Sweet, "don't ever, ever come back!"

"Not ever, Mama?" Rose cried.

"Not ever!" Sarah screamed.

"Then I guess this is goodbye," Rose said, with tears streaming down her face. She got down on her knees next to Sarah and kissed her mother's forehead. "I love you, Mama."

"Rose, my beautiful flower, please don't leave me!" Sarah begged. "Iris and I will help you raise your baby."

"We got to go, Rose," Mr. Charlie Sweet said, before she could change her mind. "That storm is moving our way." He then stuffed his bloody handkerchief into his back pocket. He took Rose's hand

and helped her to her feet while simultaneously looking directly into Sarah's sad and defeated eyes. He suddenly felt the urge to heal the distress and disappointment he saw in the mirror of Sarah's soul. "Goodbye, Miss Sarah. I promise to love and care for Rose and your grandchild for the rest of my life."

Sarah continued to lie on the floor. As Iris looked through the window, tears began to flow down her face. The rain quickly washed them away as she stood drenched and stunned at what she was hearing. Iris was unable to move from the chair. Her aunt, Rose, was going away. Would she ever see her again?

Holding hands, Rose and Mr. Charlie Sweet hurried out the front door. They dashed across the yard and got into his old Pontiac. Mr. Charlie threw Rose's suitcase in the back seat. He started his engine and began to drive away, but abruptly stopped. He kept the motor running while Rose rolled down her window and screamed, "Iris! Iris!"

Iris jumped down from the chair. She was soaked with rain and tears. Iris ran up to the car window to find Rose crying and wiping her teary eyes with Sarah's lace handkerchief. Rose and Iris reached for each other through the open window and tightly hugged.

"Please, don't go, Aunt Rose," Iris begged. "Please, don't go. I love you."

"I love you, too, Iris!" Rose cried. "But, I also love Charlie. One day, you'll understand when you fall in love. Tell Lilly and Cleo that I love them and no matter what Mama says, we'll see each other again."

"Baby, that storm is moving our way," Mr. Charlie Sweet interrupted. "We got to get going." Then, he sped away, pulling Iris and Rose apart.

Sarah came running out of the house, over to where Iris was standing. Sarah yelled loudly at their moving car, "I'm sorry, Rose! I didn't mean it! Please don't go!"

But it was too late for them to hear her pleas. Sarah and Iris watched as Mr. Charlie Sweet drove away into the night, taking Rose and the storm with him down the bumpy, dirt road. They silently stared down the road until the Pontiac was out of their sight.

"Will she take care of herself?" Sarah asked. "Will we ever see her again?"

"She will… and we will see her again," Iris said as they walked back toward the house.

"But, when?" Sarah asked sadly.

* * * * *

Iris could hear Sarah crying throughout the night. She felt sorry for her grandmother. Rose was her favorite daughter, but Sarah was a proud and stubborn woman. The last thing she wanted from anyone was pity.

Besides, Iris was also in mourning. She had lost her innocence to a child molester, her doll to a hole in the wall, her best friend to a lie, and now her aunt to a white man.

All she really had left was her mother, Lilly, her grandmother, Sarah, and her uncle, Cleo.

CHAPTER 7

As the weeks passed, Iris and Sarah went on with their usual activities. They were pretending that everything was the same. Cleo was still hunting in the woods and Lilly was away working. Iris was hoping that Rose would, one day, be waiting for her when she got home from school like she used to. But, it never came to pass.

On one particular morning, Sarah did not feel like being alone. Instead of letting Iris get dressed and go to school, Sarah insisted that she come and keep her company at work. To persuade Iris, Sarah promised her that she could eat as many teacakes and dill pickles and drink as many sodas as she fancied from Mr. James' store. Iris jumped at the opportunity. Moreover, she could use a day away from Mrs. Cora Mae.

When they arrived at Mr. James' store, Sarah unlocked the door. She and Iris then went inside. On the counter were a glass jar of jumbo dill pickles and a cookie jar filled with Sarah's mouth-watering teacakes.

Iris' mouth began to salivate as she sat at the counter admiring all the goodies she was going to eat. As Iris pondered which snack she would devour first, Sarah cooked and carried Mr. James a bowl of oatmeal into his room.

Iris began her feast with a dill pickle, followed by a grape soda. She was just about to take her first sip when she heard Sarah scream. Iris quickly ran into Mr. James' room to find Sarah standing at the head of his bed. The bowl of oatmeal was spilled on the floor. Mr. James was staring straight ahead. His eyes were not blinking and his lips were dark blue.

"Is he dead?" Iris asked.

"As dead as a doorknob," Sarah responded.

Mr. James was the first dead person Iris had ever seen. It was strange; but even stranger was the gold coffin that sat in the corner of his bedroom. He had pre-purchased his own casket and kept it in his room for when he died.

There was a letter, among many bottles of medicine, on Mr. James' nightstand. It was addressed to Dr. Robert Baxter. However, Sarah took the liberty of reading it aloud.

"I give Sarah Jackson the house where she currently lives and my last living mule. Under my pillow is three hundred dollars for Dr. Baxter to bury me. If anybody wants my bag of money, good luck trying to find it."

Although Iris did not know much about Mr. Parker James, he was as close to a grandfather as she ever had. When Sarah was too tired to walk, he would ride her to work on his mule. Mr. James would often sit in the swing, on the front porch, with Iris while he waited for Sarah to get ready. Sometimes, he would either give Iris a stick of peppermint candy or a nickel to clean up his mule's dung.

When Sarah was ready, she and Mr. James would mount his mule and ride back to his store. Nothing looked stranger than a white man and a colored woman riding down Main Street on the back of a mule. When Iris was sure they were out of sight, she would dump the candy, along with the dung, into Sarah's flower garden to fertilize the roses. Iris did not want to eat candy that the shriveled old Mr. James had slobbered on.

"Do you want me to go and get Dr. Baxter?" Iris asked.

"You go on to school," Sarah said. "I'll take care of things here."

"Yes, ma'am," Iris replied. "Are you sure you don't want me to get the doctor or stay with you?"

Sarah insisted that Iris follow her instructions and go to school. She waved her out of Mr. James' room. "Promise me you won't tell anyone that Mr. James is dead," Sarah pleaded. "I have a few things I must take care of before anyone else knows."

Iris agreed before rushing out the door to school.

* * * * *

After the judge authenticated Mr. James' letter, Sarah inherited the last of his many mules and the deed to the house that she had lived in for so many years. She renamed the mule Sue in honor of the mule she had ridden on the back of when she first came to live with Mr. Parker James as a young girl.

Sarah eventually sold Sue to Reverend Wade Crowder for twenty dollars. As Mr. James requested, Dr. Baxter used the three hundred dollars for his burial.

In death, Mr. James had dared people to find his money. The townspeople ransacked his grocery store in search of it. But despite tearing holes in the walls and pulling up floorboards, his money was never found.

CHAPTER 8

With Rose gone, Mr. James dead, and Iris in school—Sarah was basically alone. She had begun to long for more company. She asked Lilly to quit her job and move back in with her and Iris. Lilly would not only be company for Sarah, but she could also manage the deserted house that Sarah recently purchased, using the money she saved from the sales of Cleo's furs. The house sat on top of old cement blocks. Sarah was converting it into a café for Cleo. It would be named Cleo's Place.

The new café was three houses down from Mrs. Cora Mae's school. Although it was Cleo's, he had no intention of staying at home to manage his new establishment. He only wanted to continue hunting, fishing, trapping, and collecting wild ginseng that Sears and Roebuck often purchased from him.

Lilly gladly accepted Sarah's offer because she was tired of slaving for white folks and being disrespected by their bratty children. Lilly gave Iris an after-school job as a cashier at Cleo's Place so she could spend more time with her. Iris took care of the money while Lilly cooked and served the food.

The town's colored people were excited to have a new place to congregate besides church. The conversations were loud and the jukebox music was even louder. The food was greasy, but tasty. And there was plenty of corn whiskey for everyone to drink.

* * * * *

Mrs. Cora Mae was extremely pleased with how well her students had grown into young teenagers. To show her appreciation, she announced that she was giving them a party the following Friday evening. Not only did she agree to let the girls bring their boyfriends, but she would also provide them with a live band to play some of their favorite music.

Since Iris was an A+ student and never gave Sarah or Lilly any sass, they did not object to her attending the dance. Sarah went to one of the best shops in Crosstown and paid cash for a beautiful green taffeta dress and a pair of white patent leather pumps for Iris to wear.

Iris was embarrassed to attend the dance without a boyfriend, but boys never showed any interest in dating her after the rumor of her and Annie's escapade spread around town. No one except Belinda Boggs dared to be her friend. Iris and Belinda became instant best friends because they both were constantly teased.

Belinda was an albino who wore thick eyeglasses and could not tolerate too much sunlight on her extremely pale skin. She lived in the country and wore handmade clothes sown by her mother, Emma.

Iris begged Belinda to go to the dance with her. Although Belinda did not want to go, she agreed because she did not want to disappoint her only friend. She said that she would ask her parents, Emma and Henry, and if they agreed, she would let Iris know the following day.

The next morning, Iris waited impatiently on the school steps for Belinda to arrive. As usual, Belinda would get dropped off at school in an old automobile. The car would drive up to the front of the schoolhouse, drop Belinda off, and quickly speed away. Iris anxiously watched as Belinda approached.

"Well, did your parents say you could go to the dance?"

"They said I could, only because my brother is playing in the band."

"Great!"

"But, will you be there early so I won't be by myself?"

"I promise… I'll be waiting at the front door. The dance starts at seven o'clock. I'll be there way before then."

* * * * *

The night of the dance was one of the busiest Friday's for the café. To be sure she would be on time, Iris decided to take her new dress and shoes to work so she could get dressed in the small room where Cleo slept when he was not trapping in the woods.

The café was filled with a lot of hungry and intoxicated people. Lilly was busy cooking and taking orders. Iris did not realize how late it was getting. The dance started at seven o'clock and it was already seven thirty. Cleo was late getting to the café to relieve Iris from her shift. He, however, arrived just in time to stop a fight between a wife and her husband's mistress.

Iris rushed to Cleo's room to get dressed. She removed the fried chicken and catfish smelling clothes she had been wearing all day. She used her apron to rub the sweaty odor from under her armpits. She then put on her new green taffeta dress and white pumps. Instead of combing her long black hair into a ponytail, she let it hang freely below her shoulders. She painted her lips with some red lipstick that she had taken from Lilly's pocketbook. She then took a long, hard look in the mirror and was pleased with what she saw.

Iris tried to make her way through the crowded café without being noticed, but she was unsuccessful. Drunken men, young and old, began to make catcalls at her. When Joe Kelly and his brother, Jerry, joined in the teasing—it caused everyone in the café to look in her direction.

"Hey Jerry... look at Iris," Joe said. "Doesn't she look pretty?"

"That's not the same Iris we just saw a few minutes ago," Jerry answered.

"She's even wearing lipstick," Joe added.

"Fools," Lilly said, "stop teasing my daughter."

"I'm not teasing your daughter," Joe said. "She looks good!"

"Joe Kelly, don't embarrass my niece," Cleo said. "Have some respect or get the hell out of my café."

"You heard my brother," Lilly intervened. "Act like you have some sense or leave!"

"I damn sure will," Joe said. "I don't need you or your café."

His brother Jerry joined their conversation and said, "Stop it Joe! Don't embarrass yourself! Everybody is looking at you. Leave Iris alone. She's a good girl."

"You're right," Joe said, embarrassed. "Iris, I'm sorry. It was the whiskey talking. You know me and Jerry have the highest respect for the Jackson family."

"Forget about it man," Cleo said. "I know you was just talking shit, but don't tease my niece again. Fooling with you is going to cause her to be late for the dance." Cleo then looked at Iris and said, "Come on so I can drive you to the schoolhouse."

"Have a good time, baby," Lilly hollered to Iris as she watched her hurry out the door. "You look so pretty! After the dance, I'll be here waiting for you!"

Cleo then drove Iris the short distance to Mrs. Cora Mae's school. He stopped his Model-T Ford directly in front of the entrance and Iris quickly ran inside. She briefly greeted Mrs. Cora Mae, who was guarding the front door.

Mrs. Cora Mae's school used to consist of only one room. However, thanks to the army donating old, unused army barracks to colored schools, she now had two extra rooms. She adjoined two army barracks, one on each side of her original one-room school. She held the party inside one of them. This gave the three-member band enough space to play their guitars and afforded the twelve girls, and their dates, with an area to socialize and dance. Two large jugs of ice-cold lemonade, little paper cups, and a platter of teacakes sat on Mrs. Cora Mae's desk.

Many of the girls were huddled around drinking lemonade and eating teacakes. The popular twins, Hattie and Mattie Jones, were dancing with their boyfriends. Iris felt deserted when she did not see Belinda.

Iris found an isolated corner and hoped to become invisible amongst the small crowd. Suddenly, she saw her uncle, Cleo, standing at the front door with Mrs. Cora Mae, who was pointing towards her. From where Iris stood, she could see the Jones' twins pointing and laughing at her uncle. Although embarrassed, Iris found the courage to leave her hiding place and to go and see what he wanted.

"What time do you want me to come back?" Cleo asked loudly.

"I think ten o'clock," Iris whispered. "I can ask Mrs. Cora Mae to be sure."

"Don't ask that bitch nothing," Cleo muttered, ensuring that Mrs. Cora Mae could not hear his insult. "I'll just come back at ten o'clock."

After Cleo left, Iris went back to stand in her corner. She briefly wished she had left with her uncle. She pressed her back against the wood planks, feeling the splinters against her skin. She carefully looked around the room in hopes of seeing her best friend. Suddenly, Iris spotted Belinda hiding behind one of the guitar players. At first glance, Iris thought the guitar player was a white boy. Belinda was looking pathetic in her flowered dress and black, rundown pumps. She had a red rose, made out of crepe paper, in her wiry blonde hair.

Iris beckoned for Belinda to come over to where she was standing, but Belinda could not budge due to fear. Iris mustered up the courage to walk over to where she was, just as the band played one last song before their break.

Two of the band members went over to drink lemonade and jive with the girls, while the handsome guitar player talked with Belinda. Iris was briefly jealous and wondered why such a handsome fellow chose to converse with Belinda instead of the other, more popular, girls attending the dance.

"Iris!" Belinda said excitedly. "This is my brother, Samuel! Sam, this is my best friend, Iris Jackson."

"Hi," Iris said shyly, relieved that the handsome Sam, and not one of the other scruffy-looking band members, was Belinda's brother.

"We call him Sam," Belinda said.

"So you're Iris Jackson?" Sam asked. "The one I see every morning waiting for Belinda?"

"I guess so," Iris replied, feeling foolish.

"Iris is my best friend," Belinda repeated.

"I know! I heard you the first time," Sam said. "Iris, you can call me Sam, too. Where's your date?"

"I don't have one," Iris said, embarrassed.

"A pretty girl like you should have a boyfriend," Sam said, flirting. "Who's going to take you home after the dance?"

"My uncle, Cleo, is coming for me. That's his café down the street."

"Me and Belinda can drop you off. We pass it on our way home."

"I guess it will be all right if your sister is with me," Iris responded.

"Great… our break is almost over," Sam said as he prepared to play the last set for the night. "I'll see you girls after the dance."

Iris and Belinda went to stand behind Mrs. Cora Mae's desk with the other shy girls. Iris silently prayed that the dance would end before ten o'clock so her uncle, Cleo, would not return to take her home and spoil her chances of riding with Sam and Belinda.

At nine-thirty, Mrs. Cora Mae walked to the middle of the room and signaled for the band to stop playing. She announced that the dance was now over. Mrs. Cora Mae was in a hurry for the attendees to leave because she only had an hour left before she would catch a train to Detroit. She was going to visit her daughter, Evelyn, and granddaughter, Annie.

Mrs. Cora Mae finished the school year with a bang. As the party was ending, she giddily told the girls that she expected to see them, back at school, during the fall. Mrs. Cora Mae then rushed them, and their dates, out of the school. The attendees began to hurry out of the building, leaving Iris and Belinda behind to wait for Sam and his band to gather their equipment.

"Iris," Mrs. Cora Mae asked, "how are you getting home?"

"Belinda and her brother are taking me," Iris answered. "Sam is going to drive me to my uncle's café where my mama is working."

"Young lady," Mrs. Cora Mae said sternly, "make sure you go directly there and no place else!"

"Yes, ma'am," Iris replied.

"Sam, don't you keep your sister out too late," Mrs. Cora Mae said.

"I won't," Sam replied.

After the band packed up their equipment—Belinda, Iris, and Sam walked to his old car. He carefully laid his guitar in his trunk before opening the front passenger door for Iris. Belinda quickly jumped in the front seat.

"Sis, can Iris ride up front and you sit in the back?" Sam asked.

"Why?" Belinda asked. "I was up here first."

"Please," Sam begged. "You can have the front seat on the ride home."

"Okay," Belinda said, pouting. "Iris, you can sit up front."

"Thanks, Sis," Sam said.

Iris nervously sat in the passenger seat while trying to avoid looking at the handsome Sam. On their ride to Cleo's Place, Sam and Iris did not utter one word to each other. Iris pretended that she was not interested in him. When she would try to steal a quick glance, Sam would always catch her and smile.

Belinda was exhausted and already asleep when Sam arrived at the café. Lilly and Cleo had closed for the night and were sitting on the stoop. Iris could see the surprised look on their faces when she stepped out of Sam's car.

"Iris, why are you here already?" Lilly asked. "It's not ten o'clock yet."

"The dance ended early," Iris replied.

"I don't remember you leaving here with this boy," Lilly said. "And why is Belinda in the backseat of that car asleep?"

"Lilly, please!" Cleo interrupted. "Give Iris and the boy a chance to speak!"

"Well, speak up!" Lilly demanded.

"I'm Samuel Boggs. Belinda is my sister."

"I know a Jim Boggs who owns a small grocery store, but he's a redneck," Cleo said.

"That's my uncle," Sam admitted. "He's my father's twin brother."

"Oh… I put my foot in my mouth," Cleo replied.

"My daddy is white and my mama is half-white," Sam responded.

"Well," Cleo said, "if you have one ounce of colored blood in your body, you're colored."

"Yes, sir." Sam agreed. "I'm proud to be colored. There's strength in color."

"Now you're preaching the gospel! I'm Cleo and this is Lilly, Iris' mother."

"Nice to meet you Miss Lilly and Mr. Cleo," Sam said. Feeling somewhat awkward, he then said, "It's getting late. I'd better get my little sister home before my mama and daddy begin to worry."

"Thanks for giving her a ride," Lilly replied.

"You're welcome, Miss Lilly." As Sam prepared to leave, he turned and said, "Nice meeting you, Iris."

"Nice meeting you, too," Iris said, trying not to blush. Glancing in the backseat and seeing that Belinda was still soundly asleep, Iris said, "Tell Belinda that I hope we see each other before school starts back."

"You will," Sam replied confidently. "I'll see to it!"

After Sam and Belinda left, Cleo drove Lilly and Iris home. Lilly sat in the front seat while Iris sat in the back. The only thing that occupied Iris' mind was Sam. She wondered, "Does Sam like me? Did I make a fool of myself? Did Lilly and Cleo embarrass him with all of their questions? Will he want to see or talk to me ever again?"

"Lilly," Cleo said, "that Samuel Boggs seems like a nice fellow."

"He does have good manners," Lilly replied. "What do you think, Iris?"

Iris heard her question, but was too engulfed in her thoughts to respond.

"You're mighty quiet back there," Cleo said sarcastically. "Are you thinking about S-A-M-U-E-L?"

"I believe she's been bitten by the love bug," Lilly joked.

When they reached home, Cleo walked them to the front porch. As they waited for Sarah to open the door, Lilly reminded Cleo that he would only have to drive her to work in the morning because Iris was staying home to help Sarah with the housework.

Recognizing that it would only be a few more hours before it was time to take Lilly back to work, Cleo decided to stay the night in lieu of driving back to the café, sleeping in his small room, and returning again in the morning.

When Sarah opened the door, Iris rushed inside and prepared for bed. The aroma of Sarah's freshly baked sweet potato pie filled the air. Cleo and Lilly followed Sarah into the kitchen where she cut them a slice.

"This pie sure is good," Lilly said.

As Cleo took small bites of it, he said, "Mama, I'll soon have a big surprise to announce to you and Lilly."

"What is it Cleo?" Sarah asked.

"I hope it's good news," Lilly added.

"Y'all will just have to wait and see," Cleo responded. "Besides…

it's getting late and Lilly and I have to get up early."

Iris could hear Sarah, Lilly, and Cleo talking as she slipped on her nightgown. But, none of their conversation was of any importance or concern to her. All she wanted to do was go to sleep and dream about Sam.

CHAPTER 9

Iris awoke to the sweet scent of peach blossoms coming through the open windows. A few years ago, Sarah had planted peach trees in their backyard and they were in bloom. Iris sat up in her bed and listened to the buzzing honeybees as they sucked nectar and gathered pollen.

Every Saturday, she and Sarah would clean the house. They would open all of the windows to air it out, sweep the floors, dust the furniture, and wash their laundry in washtubs.

If time permitted, Iris would also help Sarah pull up weeds from their vegetable and flower gardens.

Iris wished that she could stay in bed all day and soak up the sunrays that shone through her window. It would be a perfect day to reminisce about Sam and the dance. But Sarah had already begun the chores and Iris felt compelled to assist her.

She stumbled out of bed and went to the back door when she heard Sarah calling her name. Blinded by the sunlight, she could barely see Sarah scrubbing clothes on the washboard.

"Mama," Iris yelled. "Did you call me?"

"Iris," Sarah said, "I want you to go down to Mr. Jim Boggs' store and buy me twenty-five cents worth of sugar. I need some for my coffee."

When Mr. James died, his store was so ransacked by Crosstown residents in search of his money that it eventually had to be demolished. That left the Boggs' Grocery Store as the only alternative for local shopping.

For Iris, going to the store to buy sugar was far easier than cleaning the house and washing clothes. She gladly put on an old housedress and in her bare feet, uncombed hair, and last night's lipstick—headed out of the house.

Iris was almost in sight of the store when she heard someone calling her name. She turned around and saw Sam walking towards her. Although she was embarrassed about her appearance, Iris waited for him to catch up to her. She felt as though her heart was going to jump out of her chest at any moment.

"I must've just missed you. I just stopped by your house and your grandmother told me you were going to Boggs' to buy her some sugar," Sam said as they walked toward the store.

"Where's your car?"

"I left it parked at your house. Do you mind if I walk with you?"

"I guess not. How did you know where I lived?"

"Belinda told me after I dropped you off at the café last night."

"Did you make up that story about Mr. Jim Boggs being your daddy's twin brother?"

"No, it's true. Uncle Jim hasn't spoken to my daddy since he married my mama. Even though we've been in his store before, he doesn't even know who Belinda and me are. Uncle Jim thinks I'm just another white boy around town." Sam then paused before asking, "Can I come and see you sometime?"

"That's fine with me… but, you'll have to ask my grandmother for permission," Iris said, not wanting to sound too anxious.

"I'll ask Miss Sarah just as soon as we get back to your house!"

When Iris and Sam entered the back door of the grocery store, the white men and women stopped their chatting and stared at them before proceeding with their shopping.

Mr. Jim Boggs was chewing tobacco and spitting in a spittoon as he served customers. Some of his tobacco juice splattered on Iris' bare feet as she walked by. From where she stood, she could smell his bad breath.

"What do you want, gal?" Mr. Jim asked.

"A twenty-five cent bag of sugar," Iris answered.

"Can you say P-L-E-A-S-E?" Mr. Jim said as he looked around the store for the white customers' approval.

"Yes, sir," Iris answered, embarrassed by the white customers giggling at her.

"Then let me hear you say it," Mr. Jim demanded.

"A twenty-five cent bag of sugar… please," Iris replied.

"That's better," Mr. Jim said. "What's your name gal?"

"Iris Jackson, sir."

"Are you Sarah Jackson's grand gal?" Mr. Jim asked.

"Yes, sir." Iris answered.

"Sarah Jackson is that white-looking, colored woman who used to work for old man Parker James all those years," Mr. Jim added.

Then one of his customers asked him, "Did anybody ever find Parker James' sack of money?"

"I don't know," Mr. Jim answered. "If you ask me, I believe Sarah got that money."

"Me, too," another customer chimed in.

"I wouldn't be surprised if Parker James gave his money to his nigger woman," Mr. Jim said. "I heard there was something more between him and Sarah than just boss and maid. They say he was the daddy of her children." Mr. Jim then turned his attention to Sam and asked, "Hey boy... what do you want?"

"Nothing, sir."

"Are you with this colored gal?" Mr. Jim asked.

"Yes, sir."

"Who are you?" Mr. Jim asked. "You look familiar to me."

"Samuel Boggs, sir. I'm your twin brother's son."

"My brother, Henry?" Mr. Jim asked, surprised.

"Yes, sir," Sam replied. "He's my father."

Mr. Jim looked around the store to see if anyone was listening. When everyone pretended to be minding their own business, he put his face so close to Sam's face that their noses almost touched. Mr. Jim squinted his eyes as he took a closer look. In Sam's face, he saw the mirror image of himself and his twin brother, Henry, whom he had not spoken to or seen in years.

"Keep quiet, boy," Mr. Jim said in a low whisper. "Don't ruin my business by letting these God-fearing, good, white folks know my nephew has nigger blood running through his veins! They'll never shop here again!"

Mr. Jim nervously grabbed a brown paper bag of sugar and dropped it into Iris' hands. She barely caught it before it almost dropped on the floor.

"You two half-breeds get this sugar, leave my quarter on the counter, and get the hell out of my store," Mr. Jim said tersely under his breath.

Mr. Jim could not let go of the racism and hatred he had for Sam and Belinda's mother, Mrs. Emma. She was once a maid and cook for the Boggs family before Mr. Henry fell in love with her. Disobeying his family's wishes, he married her. Henry and Emma got married in a neighboring town where no one knew that she was colored. After marrying, they returned to Crosstown to live in a house that they built on the Boggses' land. Although Henry's family still despised Emma, they could not prevent him from utilizing his share of their land that he owned.

As Iris and Sam left the store, he told her that he would not tell his father about what had happened in his uncle's store. Iris also agreed that she would not tell her grandmother. Sarah sometimes had an explosive temper and Iris knew that if she found out how Mr. Jim had spoken to her that she would confront him. They promised to keep the humiliation they had just endured to themselves.

When Iris and Sam entered the house, Sarah was standing over the hot, wood-burning stove. She was pouring herself a cup of freshly brewed coffee. Sam set the small bag of sugar on the kitchen table. Sarah immediately put two teaspoons of sugar into her coffee and sat down. Sam sat down at the table next to her.

"Mama… this is Sam," Iris said nervously. "He's Belinda's brother."

"We met this morning. Lilly and Cleo told me all about him last night. So you're Belinda Boggs' brother?"

"Yes, ma'am."

"Iris, you never told us Belinda had a brother."

"I didn't know until last night at the dance."

"Belinda is very shy," Sam said. "Unless you ask, she won't talk about us."

"What's your mama and daddy's first name?" Sarah asked.

"Henry and Emma. I hope you didn't mind me leaving my car parked in your yard."

"Not at all, especially since I know you're Belinda's brother," Sarah responded.

"Miss Jackson, can I come and court Iris?"

"You don't waste any time do you, boy?" Sarah responded.

"No, ma'am," Sam answered.

"How old are you, Sam?" Sarah asked.

"Eighteen."

"Four years older than Iris," Sarah said, shocked. "Iris, do you want to court Sam?"

"Yes ma'am," Iris answered, shyly.

"You can come here on either a Saturday or Sunday to visit with Iris for two hours and not a minute more! But, she can't leave the house with you until I get to know you better."

"That's fine, Miss Sarah. What about every Sunday at two o'clock?"

"Is that okay with you, Iris?" Sarah asked.

"Yes, ma'am," Iris replied, looking down at the floor.

"That will be fine, Sam," Sarah said.

"Thank you, Miss Sarah," Sam said, smiling. "Well… I guess I'll see you tomorrow, Iris."

CHAPTER 10

After Sarah stopped taking in boarders, she converted the spare bedroom into a parlor where she could entertain guests. However, she never had a guest until Sam began to date Iris.

Every Sunday—Sam, Iris, and Sarah would sit in the parlor. Sam and Sarah would do all the talking while Iris listened. When Sam's allotted two hours were over, Sarah and Iris would walk him to the door and wave him goodbye.

Sunday after Sunday, it was the same routine. But on one particular Sunday, Sarah waited in the parlor while Iris walked Sam to the door alone. After making sure that Sarah was not eavesdropping, Sam gave Iris a quick peck on her lips. The kiss felt so wonderful to Iris that she thought she would faint.

From that evening onward, Sarah let Iris and Sam spend their two hours alone. On one visit, Sam asked her if he could take Iris to his house to meet his parents. Sam must have made a great impression on Sarah because she quickly agreed.

On the Sunday that she was scheduled to meet Sam's parents, Iris was out of bed by the break of dawn. She wanted to look her prettiest for her first date outside of the house with Sam. Iris decided to wear her white dress with the black satin sash, red fox stockings, and black pumps. She was already dressed and ready an hour early.

Iris pranced back and forth, looking out of the window while Sarah was cooking breakfast. Sam eventually arrived, driving his father's old Desoto that he had freshly washed and shined. He was neatly dressed in black pants, a white shirt, and cowboy boots. Sarah was the first person Sam spoke to when he entered the house.

"Good morning, Miss Sarah. Mama and Daddy said to thank you for letting Iris visit them. My mama has been cooking since early this morning and Belinda can't wait to see her."

"That's great, Sam. Just don't forget to have Iris back home before six o'clock."

"I promise," Sam assured her.

"Iris, don't you and Sam want to eat breakfast before y'all go?"

"No, ma'am," Iris answered.

"Sam," Sarah asked, "what about you?"

"No, ma'am," Sam answered. "My family is eager to see Iris. We'd better get going."

Before Sarah could say another word, Sam ushered Iris out of the door and into his car. Through the rearview mirror, Iris could see Sarah standing on the porch, watching them, as they drove away.

After turning off of the main highway, onto a deserted country road, it felt like they had been riding for miles. They drove past fallen houses, some burned down to the ground with only the chimneys still standing, and acres of abandoned fields where cotton once grew and was picked by slaves. Iris wondered, "What happened to the people who once lived in all those dilapidated houses? Where have they gone?"

Sam finally arrived at his house, nestled deep in the woods. A skinny albino woman, whom Belinda resembled, and a tall white man, who was the identical twin of Mr. Jim Boggs, stood on the raggedy porch.

Sam parked his car under a huge birch tree. He and Iris walked across the broom swept yard and up the rickety steps to meet his family.

"Mom and Dad, this is Iris, my future wife," Sam gushed.

Iris was speechless, not expecting Sam's introduction.

"Welcome to our home," Mrs. Emma said.

"Glad you could come," Mr. Henry said. "Sam was right. You're a pretty little thing."

"She sure is and her hair is so long," Mrs. Emma agreed, sliding her fingers through Iris' long ponytail, causing her to shy away.

Mr. Henry had dried spit from chewing tobacco on his mouth, overalls, and red plaid shirt. His boots were worn down to the soles due to working in the fields. On the contrary, Mrs. Emma had such pride about herself. Although faded, her blue dress was clean and ironed. She smelled of vanilla extract. Her beautiful face, however, looked tired and wrinkled as though she had lived through some hard times.

The Boggses led Iris down a narrow hallway into the kitchen where Belinda was setting the table. Sam's old hound dog was stretched out underneath it. Belinda, wearing the same dress she had worn to the school dance, was overjoyed to see her best friend for the first time in months.

The kitchen table was set with bowls and platters of fried chicken, stewed squirrel, collard greens cooked in fatback, potato salad, salt-water cornbread, and sweet potato pies.

Mr. Henry sat down at the table before Mrs. Emma. Sam waited until all the women were seated before joining them. Mr. Henry mumbled some quick words of prayer and ended it with, "Amen! Now… let's eat." They began to pass around the platters and bowls until each of their plates was filled to capacity.

"Iris, do you want some more cornbread?" Mrs. Emma asked.

"Yes, ma'am," Iris answered.

"Henry, pass the cornbread to Iris," Mrs. Emma said.

"It's closer to you," Mr. Henry responded through a mouthful of food.

"I'll get it, Mama," Sam said.

After dinner, Mr. Henry fell asleep on the back porch with tobacco juice running down the corners of his mouth.

Sam and Iris stepped over his snoring body in order to EXIT the house. Sam took a blanket off of the clothesline and carried it under his arm. They then walked down to the creek. The hound dog wagged his tail behind them until Sam ordered him to go back to the house.

"What's your dog's name?" Iris asked.

"Dog," Sam answered.

"What's his name?" Iris asked again, thinking Sam had not heard her correctly.

"Dog," he repeated.

"You named your dog, Dog?" Iris asked in surprise.

"Why not name my dog, Dog?" Sam asked.

Iris shrugged her shoulders and giggled. Sam reached for her hand and laughed, also. Sam and Iris held hands as they walked far past the Boggs' house. They stopped and stood on the sandy banks of a creek that was hidden behind tall trees. It was a beautiful, romantic, and serene place. It was the perfect place for Iris to fall in love with Sam—the man who she wanted to father her children, grow old with, and be buried next to.

"What I said to my folks about you being my future wife is true," Sam said as they sat on top of the blanket he had just laid on the ground. "I love you, Iris. Will you marry me?"

"I don't know, Sam," Iris responded, looking attentively into his eyes. "It's always been my dream to graduate from high school, to go to college, and become a teacher. It's my grandmother and Lilly's dream for me, too. They are depending on me to see our dream come true. I don't want to disappoint them or myself."

"I know you have another year in high school and are dreaming of going to college and becoming a teacher," Sam said as he took a small diamond ring out of his back pocket. "When you do all of those things, then will you marry me? I'll wait for you. I've enlisted in the Army for four years. After I serve my tour of duty, you'll be finished with college and we can get married then. You can teach school while I farm and build us a home for our children. We could live right here on all this land my family owns if you want. I can build us a house right here next to this creek. This could be our sacred place. Iris, please say yes."

"If I accept, can we keep it a secret from my grandmama and Lilly?"

"I promise," Sam said, kneeling on one knee. "Will you accept this ring that once belonged to my mama's great-grandmother? Will you be my wife?"

"I love you, Sam! Yes, I'll marry you."

Sam's hands began to shake as he put the ring on Iris's finger. It fit perfectly as if it was custom made just for her. Sam sat very close to Iris and began kissing her. He was more experienced than she was. But, as they continued to kiss, Iris caught on quickly.

For a few moments, thoughts of Mr. Joe Fish came to her mind. Iris wanted to jump up and run away from Sam, but she decided that she would not let the memory of her horrible past destroy one of the best days of her present. Nor was Iris going to let it ruin her future with Sam.

She did, however, remember what Lilly once said to her about the birds and the bees when she was twelve years old. Lilly told her that she had become a woman and to be careful since she was now menstruating. At that time, Iris immaturely thought Lilly meant to be careful of birds dropping poop on her head or getting stung by bees. She also remembered her aunt, Rose's, words before leaving with Mr. Charlie Sweet about one day understanding how it would feel to be in love.

Sam laid his body on top of hers. He pressed his lips tightly against hers and ever so gently entered her vagina with his penis. Iris wanted to scream from the pleasurable pain, but she feared his parents and Belinda would hear her and come running down to the creek.

Afterwards, Sam and Iris cuddled until the sun began to set. They did not want to leave, but Sam promised Sarah that he would have her back home by six o'clock. They dusted the sand off of their clothes and blanket before rushing back to Sam's house.

Mr. Henry was still asleep on the porch. Mrs. Emma and Belinda were sitting near him in a swing. As they walked closer, Iris remained in the yard while Sam went to tell them that he was going to drive her home. Iris removed the ring from her finger and hid it inside her bra. She did not want to walk any closer to Sam's family because she feared that Mrs. Emma would somehow know what she and Sam had done. She waved goodbye, from their yard, before getting into Sam's car.

Sam and Iris sat close to each other until her house was in view. They could see Sarah standing in the same place that she was in when they left earlier that morning. It was as if Sarah had not moved all day.

"I told you, Miss Sarah," Sam said, "I'd have her back by six."

"Yes, you did," Sarah said. "Iris, the dirty dishes are waiting for you to wash them," giving Sam a clue that it was time for him to leave.

"Yes, ma'am," Iris said.

"I'd better be going," Sam said, taking the hint.

"See you next Sunday, Iris," Sam said as he got back into his car. "Goodbye, Miss Sarah."

"Goodbye, Sam," Sarah responded.

After Sam left, Iris began to wash the dishes. Sarah sat at the kitchen table, drinking a glass of ice tea. Iris was hoping that Sarah would not question her about her day, but her hopes were to no avail.

"Iris, did you let Sam get between your legs?"

"No, Mama," Iris said defiantly before again exclaiming, "No!"

"You're lying, Iris. You're not my same little, sweet girl who left here this morning. I can tell by just looking at you. Sam has taken away your innocence and your dream of being the first in our family to be somebody."

“Mama, Sam loves me. He wouldn’t do anything to hurt me.”

“I hope you’re right, but sometimes love isn’t enough,” Sarah said sternly. “I feel a cold wind in your future.”

Sarah left Iris washing the dishes while she went into her bedroom to lie across the bed. She would often do that if she felt troubled.

The thought of Sarah’s words sent chills through Iris’ body. Too often, her predictions had come true. But, Iris was determined to prove that Sarah’s belief that Sam was going to be another no-good cheater and deserter, like all the men had been in her life, would not come true.

Iris wanted to know when Sarah’s mistrust in men had begun. Had it begun with Sarah’s father who abandoned her as an infant? Mr. Parker James, who fathered her children and treated her as nothing more than his slave? George Dawson, the man she briefly dated before he molested Lilly and hid from the law at Mrs. Cora Mae’s house? Or Mr. Joe Fish, the boarder who had run away with her money and, unbeknownst to her, had molested her granddaughter?

Iris reasoned that Sarah was entitled to her feelings of mistrust. She stopped washing dishes and laid the dishcloth in the sink. She then went to talk with Sarah. Iris wanted to know more about her mysterious grandmother.

“Mama, are you asleep? Mama, are you asleep?” Iris repeated.

“No.” Sarah finally responded.

“I was just wondering, what was your mama and daddy’s names and do you have any brothers and sisters?” Iris asked.

Sarah was silent. When she did not answer, Iris knew it was not safe to badger her. Even at her age, it was not beyond possibility for Sarah to give her a slap across the face.

"I don't remember much about my mama or her people," Sarah abruptly answered. "All I know is that they looked white. I know absolutely nothing about my father. I don't know his name and I don't ever remember seeing him. But, I'll never forget the colored family, Abraham and Mabel Green, who my mama and two uncles gave me to. One of my uncles was called Billy and I can't remember my other uncle's name. But, I'll always remember my mother's name. It was Rose. I named your aunt, Rose, after her."

"Early one morning," Sarah continued, "when I was five or six years old, my two uncles and my mama took me for a ride in a wagon that was pulled by two mules. I thought we were going to pick wild blackberries for a pie, but not this time. We traveled far down a country road until we came to a small shack where Abraham and Mabel lived. My uncles and Mama left me waiting in the wagon while they went inside to talk to them."

Sarah sighed, "When they returned to the wagon, Abraham and Mabel were with them. My mama was crying. My uncle, Billy, lifted me out of the wagon and stood me beside my mama. Through tears, my mother told me that I was not going back home with her; I was going to stay and live with Abraham and Mabel. She said, 'I love you, Sarah, and don't ever forget your mama, Rose.' She then put a small diamond ring on my finger, but my uncle, Billy, took it off and kept it. He said that the ring should stay in their white family. They all got back in the wagon and rode away with my mama still crying. I tried to run behind them, but Mrs. Mabel, who always dressed in all black clothing like she was in mourning, stopped me. My mama didn't even kiss me goodbye."

Sarah, visibly traumatized, said, "Mabel worked me like a slave from sun-up to sun-down. I cleaned their filthy house. I even cooked their meals although I was only allowed to eat the leftover crumbs.

I worked in their fields, planted their vegetables, and picked their cotton. I fed the cows, the horses, and the pigs. Sometimes, I just wanted to die! Mabel was a cold-hearted woman who never spoke to me unless she was telling me what to do! She never touched me unless she was giving me a whipping! I slept in a closet on top of old dirty rags. Sometimes, late at night, Abraham would slip me some extra food."

"Mama," Iris asked tearfully, "how long did you live with those awful people?"

"I lived with Abraham and Mabel for seven or eight years until one day a creepy, old white man came riding by on his mule," Sarah answered. "Abraham was in the yard chopping firewood when the old man stopped to let his mule drink from the water trough. I was in the garden, cutting okra pods. Mabel was inside the house. Abraham stopped chopping wood and began talking to the stranger. To this day, I can still remember every word of their conversation.

'Hey, boy! What's your name?'

'Abraham Green, sir.'

'Abraham, I'm Mr. Parker James. I want to water my mule from your trough.'

'That'll be just fine. If you don't mind me asking, sir, where're you on your way to?'

'Back to town... I rode out here on a wagon, with that white family, down the road from here, to buy this mule. I named her Sue. Don't you think Sue is a good name for a mule?'

'Yes, sir.'

'Who's that white gal cutting that okra?'

'That's Sarah. She's not white.'

'Is she your daughter?'

'No, sir! My wife is as dark as I am.'

'Really? Where did you get her from?'

'Her folks didn't want her because her daddy was colored so they gave her to me and my wife.'

'How old is she?'

'I'm not sure, sir. She was about five when we got her. She's been with us for about six or seven years. You look like a kind man. Could you take her? She's a good girl and a hard worker. She could clean your house and maybe learn how to read and write.'

'Is your wife willing to let her go?'

'Yes, sir... I'm sure she won't mind. She never cared for her that much anyway. Excuse me, sir, I'll go in the house and get my wife.'"

Sarah was obviously distressed as she recalled her memories to Iris. She continued, "Abraham went into the house and got Mabel. Mr. James, Abraham, and Mabel stood by the water trough and talked before Abraham beckoned for me to come over. I immediately put my knife in the okra pan and left it sitting in the garden and went to see what they wanted.

'Sarah, this is Mr. Parker James,' Abraham said. 'He's thinking about taking you to town to live with him to be his cook and house-keeper.'

'Gal,' Mr. Parker James asked, 'can you keep house and cook?'

'Yes, sir!' Abraham interrupted. 'Not only is she a good field hand, but she keeps a clean house for my wife and is a darn good cook.'

'Mabel,' Mr. James asked, 'you don't mind if this here gal leaves with me?'

'I don't care,' Mabel said. 'She's not my daughter. My daughter is dead. I'll be glad to get rid of her so she can stop reminding me of my dead child.'

'Well gal," Mr. Parker James said, "it looks like you'll be coming home with me.'"

Sarah then said, "Right then, without saying goodbye, Mabel turned and went back into the house. Abraham helped me up on the mule, where I sat behind Mr. James. With just the clothes on my back and no shoes on my feet, Mr. James took me to stay with him in this very same house where you, Lilly, and me live now. I basically became his slave. Later on, he moved out of this house and into the back room of his grocery store. Some of the things Parker James made me do ain't, even at your age, for your ears to hear. Sometimes I wonder which part of my life was worse. Was it with Abraham and Mabel or with Parker James?"

"I'm sorry you had such a horrible childhood," Iris said.

"It was the times," Sarah said. "That's just the way things was then."

"Did you ever see Abraham or Mabel again?" Iris asked.

"Never saw them again!" Sarah said happily.

Sarah abruptly stopped talking and did not utter another word. She then pulled the covers over her graying head. Iris knew that Sarah, a very proud woman, wanted to nurse her wounds and cry alone. Iris pretended as though she needed to go and finish washing the dishes.

Iris instead went into the kitchen, took out the small diamond ring that she had hidden in her bra, and sat down at the table. As she stared at the ring, she had an overwhelming bittersweet feeling. On the one hand, she was engaged and in love with Sam. But on the other hand, she felt such guilt for lying to Sarah, especially after hearing her sad story.

Iris returned to the bedroom and carefully tucked her engagement ring away in her keepsake box. She undressed, put on her night-gown, and went to bed.

CHAPTER 11

Sarah and Belinda were jealous that Iris was spending most of her time with Sam and not with them. But Iris did not care because they were in love. Sarah secretly hoped that their relationship would end when Sam left for the army and Iris returned to school in the fall.

During their last days together, Iris and Sam would skip pebbles across the creek or lie on top of their special blanket while Iris read to him from one of Sarah's romance novels. They spent their last few lazy days of summer loving each other or falling asleep in each other's arms—only to be awakened by Dog licking their faces with his sticky tongue.

Sam was scheduled to leave the Sunday before Mrs. Cora Mae re-opened her school. He was leaving for eight weeks to attend basic training in Fort Hood, Texas. After that, he would return to Crosstown for only one week before being shipped overseas.

Saturday was Iris and Sam's last day together. They shared their last day with no one but Dog.

"What if..." Iris began.

"What if what?" Sam asked.

"Nothing. I just don't want you to go."

"I have to go, Iris. This is the best thing for both of us. I promise you, I'll come home safely from both Texas and overseas. A little war isn't going to keep me away from you. I love you too much."

"I love you, too."

"You do trust me, don't you?"

"I do, Sam."

"Then, let's not waste another precious second of our last day together. I only want to spend this moment with you. Nothing else matters!"

*　　*　　*　　*　　*

The Sunday morning that Sam was scheduled to leave finally arrived. Mr. Henry, Mrs. Emma, Belinda, and Iris went to the train station with Sam to buy his ticket and to see him off safely.

Iris and Sam were holding hands as they walked through the crowded train station. Mr. Henry was walking with them. Mrs. Emma, who was lagging behind with Belinda, caught up to Iris and forcefully grabbed her hand. This forced Iris to slow down, allowing Mr. Henry and Sam to continue without her.

"Iris," Mrs. Emma said, "let Sam and his daddy go to the ticket window by themselves."

Out of respect for Mrs. Emma, Iris remained behind. Nevertheless, she desperately wanted to ask Mrs. Emma why she did not want her to wait at the ticket window with them. But before Iris could utter a word, Belinda asked the question for her.

"Mama," Belinda asked, "why can't Iris go to the ticket window with Daddy and Sam?"

"You'll see why," Mrs. Emma answered. "Just watch and listen."

There was a long line of colored boys waiting to buy their tickets. It was obvious by their haircuts and duffle bags that they were young lads who were also preparing to go off to basic training. When the white clerk noticed Mr. Henry and Sam, he beckoned for the colored boys to step aside so they could purchase their tickets first. This allowed Mr. Henry and Sam to cut through the long line and go directly to the front. The colored boys did not object; they just politely stepped to the side.

Iris now understood why Mrs. Emma insisted that she not walk side-by-side with Mr. Henry and Sam. She must have feared that Iris was not light-skinned enough to pass for white. At that moment, Iris also realized why Sarah did not like dark-skinned boys around her daughters. She did not want them to get impregnated and have dark-complexioned babies. Sarah feared it would hinder her grandchildren from fully assimilating into a white man's world. In hindsight, Iris surmised that the only reason Sarah allowed her to date Sam was because he could pass for white. Though this epiphany was sobering, Iris was dismayed at the realization that colored boys could fight and die for their country, but were not deserving of the same respect as a white male.

"Mama," Belinda asked, "will we colored folks always be at the back of the line?"

"Things won't change in my lifetime, but hopefully they will in yours," Mrs. Emma replied. "Things are slowly changing and will continue to change in the years to come. But for now, as a colored person, you have to take advantage of every chance you can get."

Sam held onto his ticket as they waited for the train. Eventually, the porter announced that it was time to board the train because it would be departing in less than five minutes.

All of the colored boys were hugging their relatives and kissing their girlfriends goodbye. Some of them were even crying. Were these tears of joy or sadness? After all, many of them were just scared young boys who were leaving Crosstown for the first time. They were leaving behind the people they knew—their mothers, fathers, siblings, and friends—in search of a better life. Would they find it as soldiers in the United States Army?

Iris could sense that Sam wanted to cry, but he was determined to appear brave in front of her and his family. He said goodbye to everyone, but saved his last farewell for Iris. He hugged his mother and sister and was preparing to shake his father's hand when Mr. Henry, a man who always seemed unemotional, pulled Sam close and tightly hugged him. For once, Mr. Henry was letting Sam know that he loved him and that he was not ashamed of showing his softer side.

“Son, I want you to take care of yourself,” Mr. Henry said.

“I will, Daddy.”

“We love you, Sam,” Mrs. Emma cried.

“See you in eight weeks,” Belinda added.

Iris was feeling left out until Mr. Henry noticed her and said, “Move away from the boy so he can speak to Iris.”

“I’ll miss you, Sam,” Iris said, crying.

“Don’t cry,” Sam said as he tightly grasped her hand. “I won’t be gone long.” Noticing the train was preparing to depart, he quickly kissed her and said, “I got to go now; the train is about to leave.”

As the train began to slowly move, Sam grabbed hold of the railing and jumped on. He then waved his final goodbye.

“I love you!” Iris screamed to Sam, but it was too late for him to hear her.

Mrs. Emma, Belinda, and Iris were all crying, as was the stoic Mr. Henry. It was as if they were never going to see Sam again.

They watched the train, moving ever so slowly, until it picked up speed and disappeared around the bend.

* * * * *

A week after Sam left, Iris received her first letter from him. Inside of it was a small photo. In the picture, Sam was wearing his army uniform with dog tags hanging around his neck.

The eight weeks of Sam's basic training seemed to pass ever so slowly. But, Iris kept busy by focusing on completing her last year of school. When she would receive a letter from Sam, she would immediately write him back that same day.

Iris had started to become extremely nervous and easily angered. She cried a lot and sometimes vomited after eating. She thought that it was because she was longing Sam until she realized that she had missed her menstrual cycle.

Without giving him time to even respond to her last letter, Iris wrote Sam another one. In her letter, she wrote that she was sure that she was pregnant.

Iris finally got a reply to her last two letters. Sam wrote back telling her not to worry. He stated that if she were pregnant that they would have to change their plans and immediately get married after he returned from basic training. Sam ensured Iris that she would only have to wait another week before he would be home to visit her. He wanted to be with her when she told Sarah and Lilly the news.

Sam was sure that after their son or daughter was born, Mrs. Emma would gladly keep their child so Iris could fulfill her dreams of attending Tuskegee Institute.

For the meantime, Sam's encouraging words and unwavering support eased Iris' mind.

CHAPTER 12

Iris was overjoyed to receive her long-awaited letter from Tuskegee Institute. Mrs. Cora Mae walked over to Iris' desk and ecstatically handed it to her. She then waited for her to read it. The letter stated that Iris was accepted into its College of Education for the upcoming fall semester. Iris' dream of becoming a teacher was finally coming true.

Nevertheless, Sarah's prediction of a cold wind in Iris' future was also coming to fruition. She was now pregnant with Sam's baby. Iris would have to tell Sarah and Lilly the good news that she had been accepted into Tuskegee Institute. However, she would also have to tell them the bad news that she would not be going to college because she had to stay home in order to raise her baby. Although Iris loved Sam, at that moment, she resented him.

That evening when Iris came home from school, she read her acceptance letter to them. Lilly was so excited that she had Iris to read it again.

"My baby is going to a famous college!" Lilly said.

"I've never liked that Cora Mae," Sarah said, "but I have to give that woman credit for preparing Iris for college!"

"Come on, Mama, let's rejoice over Iris' good news," Lilly said.

Iris continued, "They said that I would be given a work-study job to help me pay for my tuition."

"I have some money saved up to help you," Sarah offered. "You just make us proud. This has been a long-awaited day for the Jackson family. I feel so happy. I think I'll go in the kitchen and make a pound cake so we can eat it with supper. Hallelujah!"

"You can say that again, Mama!" Lilly said.

"Hallelujah!" Sarah repeated.

"I'll help you in the kitchen, Mama," Lilly laughed. "Iris, you just sit right here in Mama's rocking chair and wait until supper is ready. This is your celebration meal!"

Iris was happy that she and Sam had decided to keep the news of her pregnancy from Lilly and Sarah until he returned from basic training. Until then, Sarah and Lilly could rejoice in their happiness a little while longer.

* * * * *

In a rare manifestation of prescience and as a preemptive strike against integration, the county school board had decided to build a small public school for Negro children. The school would be named Mary Hines Johnson after an educational pioneer who started the first black school in the neighboring town of Franklin, Georgia.

Consequently, Mrs. Cora Mae's school would no longer be needed. Hence, Iris' class would be the last one to graduate from there. After Iris and Belinda finished their last year, Mrs. Cora Mae would close her school and move to Detroit to live with her daughter, Evelyn, and her granddaughter, Annie. All the colored boys and girls would now be bused to the newly built school.

When the last day of school was over and all the girls except Iris and Belinda had left, Mrs. Cora Mae motioned for Iris to come up to her desk.

Iris feared, as many babies as Mrs. Cora Mae had birthed, that she might be aware of her secret. Reluctantly, with Belinda looking on, Iris got out of her seat, pulling her large sweater around her stomach, and went to stand in front of Mrs. Cora Mae's desk.

"That sweater you got tied around your waist is too hot for this weather!" Mrs. Cora Mae said. "Is there something you want to tell me?"

"No, ma'am," Iris answered.

"Now, Iris, you can't fool me! Are you pregnant? And, don't you lie to me, missy!"

"Yes, ma'am... I'm pregnant."

"Is the daddy Belinda's brother?"

"Yes, ma'am."

"Does Belinda know that you're expecting her brother's baby?"

"Yes, ma'am. Sam wrote a letter to his family and told them that I was expecting his baby."

"You mean to tell me that Lilly, your own mother, and your grandmother, Sarah, doesn't know?"

"No, ma'am."

"So, Sarah won't be having a college graduate in her family after all," Mrs. Cora Mae said, smirking.

"Please don't tell them until I do," Iris begged.

"If you don't tell Sarah or Lilly today… tomorrow, I'll just have to make a special trip to your house and tell them myself!"

"I'll tell them as soon as I get home," Iris pleaded.

"You can go on home now, Iris," Mrs. Cora Mae said. "Best of luck to you and don't forget what I just told you." She then paused before saying, "Belinda you just sit right there until your daddy comes for you."

"See you soon, Iris," Belinda said.

"Goodbye, Belinda," Iris responded as she prepared to EXIT the classroom. When she got to the door, she turned around and said, "Thank you Mrs. Cora Mae for giving us colored girls an opportunity to go to school and get an education when no one else believed in us."

"You're welcome, Iris! It's my hope that all of the colored girls that attended my school will have a bright future… including you," Mrs. Cora Mae said in a saddened voice.

Iris then went directly home. She knew that she could not wait for Sam to be with her when they announced the news of her pregnancy to Sarah and Lilly. Because of Mrs. Cora Mae, she was now forced to reveal her secret to Sarah and Lilly as soon as she arrived home.

But, Iris did not get the opportunity. As soon as she walked into the house, her grandmother was waiting for her. The first words out of Sarah's mouth were, "Iris, are you pregnant?"

"Yes, ma'am," Iris nervously admitted.

"I knew it… I knew it!" Sarah cried. "You can't fool me! I said the other day that I better face the truth and ask you before it was too late to fix your situation. Is Sam the daddy?"

"Yes, ma'am…but, let me explain our plans."

Before Iris could explain, Sarah ran out of the house in a rage. She paced back and forth on the porch, waiting for the first person to drive by so he or she could take a message to Lilly at Cleo's Place.

When Sarah saw Mr. Jack Jones driving by in his old truck, she immediately flagged him down and yelled for him to stop. He braked his car to a sudden standstill to see what she wanted.

"Jack, ride over to the café and tell Lilly to come home right away," Sarah said distraughtly. "I want you to wait for her so you can drive her back to the house."

"Is something the matter, Miss Jackson?" Jack asked.

"Mind your own damn business, Jack!" Sarah snapped. "Just do what I said! Now go!"

Complying with Sarah's request, Mr. Jack Jones quickly drove away. Sarah then stormed back into the house. She looked at Iris, who was sitting on the edge of her bed. Acting out her distress, Sarah continued to pace back and forth across the aged, wooden floor. She mumbled, "I knew something like this would happen if you continued to see that good for nothing Sam. I tried to warn Lilly, but she was too busy working at Cleo's Place to stop you from seeing that rascal. Now, it's too late!"

The worn floorboards began to buckle, even more, under the weight of Sarah's large body. Iris was afraid that the floor was going to collapse and Sarah would fall through it. That thought almost caused Iris to laugh, but she continued to sit silently and wait for Lilly to arrive.

Eventually, Lilly rushed into the house, panicking. She was still wearing her food-stained apron.

"What happened?" Lilly asked. "Mama, are you sick?"

"I'm not sick," Sarah snapped.

"Is something wrong with you, Iris?" Lilly asked.

"Tell her, Iris!" Sarah demanded.

"What happened, Iris?" Lilly yelled.

"I'll tell you, Lilly," Sarah interjected. "Iris is going to have a baby!"

"Iris is that true?" Lilly asked, dumbfounded.

"Yes, ma'am," Iris answered, looking down at the floor! "It's true."

"Iris, how could you do this to us?" Lilly asked. "How could you do this to yourself? Mama, what are we going to do?"

"I just don't know!" Sarah said. "I just don't know!"

Sarah stopped pacing the floor and sat in her rocking chair to think. Shocked by the news, Lilly sat on the bed next to Iris and began to sob.

"Please listen to me," Iris begged them. "I've already completed Mrs. Cora Mae's school. The baby should be here before I'm scheduled to leave for college. Sam has already written to his mama and told her about our situation. She wrote him back and told him that I can come and live with them. When the baby is born, his family has agreed to take care of our child while I attend college. I promise that I'm going to finish my education! When Sam is out of the army and I'm a teacher, we'll get married as planned. Mrs. Emma said that she would return our child to us when we were ready. By then, who would care about or remember what happened four years ago?"

"Well, Mama," Lilly said, agreeing, "I guess that's the best we can do for now."

"No… it's not," Sarah said. "I know someone who can take care of this problem for us."

"Mama, if you're thinking what I think you're thinking, the answer is no," Lilly said. "This baby will be your great grandchild and my grandchild. Who knows what great things this baby might accomplish in its lifetime? Besides, we're not the only people who know that Iris is pregnant. Sam knows and the Boggs know! What lie would we tell them if this baby, growing inside of Iris' stomach, just suddenly disappeared?" Lilly looked at Iris and asked, "Besides us and the Boggs, have you told anyone else?"

"Mrs. Cora Mae knows," Iris answered. "She asked me and I told her the truth. I couldn't lie to her."

“Now the whole damn town knows!” Sarah said. “That bitch is probably laughing at me now! Damn her!”

“She wished me the best of luck,” Iris responded.

“Yea... yea!” Sarah replied. “Trust me... I know that bitch better than you do!”

“Don’t worry, Iris,” Lilly said. “We’ll get through this! Somehow, we’ll make it through this!”

“Well, you and Iris will have to raise this baby,” Sarah said. “I raised my four children and I even raised you, Iris. I’m too old to start over with another child.”

“Mama,” Iris said, “if for some unforeseeable reason my and Sam’s plans don’t work out with Mr. and Mrs. Boggs, I promise you that I’ll forget college and stay home to raise my child on my own.”

“Your dreams of going to college and becoming a teacher and marrying Sam will not come to pass,” Sarah said. “I feel a cold wind deep in my bones.”

“Iris, don’t listen to Mama’s predictions,” Lilly said. “They will not come true! Not this time! God, please, not this time!”

CHAPTER 13

The war was taking a turn for the worse. More and more young men were needed to fight in Germany. The draft was in full force and many troops were being sent directly from boot camp to the battlefield. Unfortunately, Sam's unit was one of the first chosen to go.

Sam and Iris often wrote letters to each other. In their correspondence, they talked about their child's future. Even Sarah and Lilly were becoming more optimistic after Mr. and Mrs. Boggs assured them that they would take responsibility for raising the baby while Sam was in the Army and Iris was at college.

To bridge the two families and solidify their agreement, Mr. Henry and Mrs. Emma invited the Jacksons to their house for Sunday dinner. It took a lot of pleading from Lilly and Iris, but they finally convinced Sarah and even Cleo, who had unexpectedly come home from trapping in the woods, to have dinner at the Boggses.

With the Jacksons and the Boggses willing to break bread together, that particular Sunday should have been one of Iris' happiest. However, everyone seemed to be in a happy mood—except her. She felt as though gloom was hovering over her.

They all piled in Cleo's old Ford, with the food Sarah had cooked and Iris' packed suitcase, and rode to the Boggses' house. As they continued down the isolated and dusty roads—Sarah, Cleo, and Lilly chatted about the fertile and unused land.

"I've hunted in these woods many times," Cleo said. "I've always wondered who this land belongs to."

"Sam said that his family owns all of this land," Iris replied. "When Sam comes home from the army, he's going to build us a home near the creek. He's planning to grow cotton and vegetables. Farming will be his job and mine will be caring for our children and teaching school."

"I hope and pray all of your plans come true," Lilly said.

"Me too," Sarah agreed.

"I do too," Cleo said.

When the Jacksons arrived at the Boggses' house, Mr. Henry and Mrs. Emma were on their front porch making homemade ice cream in a wooden, hand-cranked, churn. Mr. Henry turned the crank on the churn while Mrs. Emma added chunks of chipped ice.

Belinda hurried out of the house to meet the Jacksons. Dog, who had been sleeping underneath the porch, stood up and barked. Then he lazily laid back down and went to sleep. Mr. Henry and Mrs. Emma stopped churning the ice cream to greet them. Mr. Henry even opened the car door for Sarah.

"Welcome, folks," Mr. Henry said. "I'm Henry Boggs and that there is my wife, Emma."

"I'm Sarah Jackson and this is my son, Cleo," Sarah said, smiling. "That's Lilly, my daughter and Iris' mother. And… I suppose I don't have to introduce you to my granddaughter, Iris."

"No, ma'am, Miss. Jackson," Mr. Henry responded. "We all know and love Iris. After all, she's going to be the mother of my grandbaby."

While the two families got better acquainted, Iris and Belinda hurried to Belinda's bedroom so they could chat.

Belinda had eight tiny nightshirts folded neatly on top of her pink chenille bedspread. She and Mrs. Emma had hand-sewn them, out of bleached flour sacks, as a gift for the baby. Next to Belinda's bed was a small crib, built by Mr. Henry.

Iris sat on Belinda's bed and admired the nightshirts. Then she carefully refolded each of them. She knew that she and Sam's baby would be loved, cared for, and safe in the hands of the Boggses.

"If you get any fatter, I'll have to let you have the whole bed and I'll have to sleep on the floor," Belinda said, looking at Iris."

"I'm not getting fat," Iris replied defensively. "It's the baby in my stomach. When it comes, I'm going to be my old skinny self again."

"Tell me, Iris," Belinda began, "did you know you could get pregnant when you and Sam were doing it?"

"I guess so."

"Then why did you do it?"

"I don't know."

"Didn't Lilly tell you about the birds and the bees?"

"Yes... I guess she didn't tell me enough because the bee that stung me gave me a ba-bee."

Belinda and Iris both laughed before continuing their conversation.

"Have you?" Iris asked.

"Have I what?"

"You know!"

"No! No!" Belinda said, interrupting. "But I want to someday. Did it feel good?"

"The more we did it, the more I liked it," Iris answered. "But, I guess it depends on the bee." She then paused before saying, "Come on and let's join our folks on the porch. After today, we'll have plenty of time to talk."

Iris and Belinda then went and sat on the porch to talk with the others. Unexpectedly, a white car drove towards the house. The words U.S.

Army were printed on the side of it.

Although Iris and Belinda did not know the significance of that white car, the demeanor of the older folks seemed to signify that it meant something serious. Mr. Henry put his arm around Mrs. Emma's shoulders and held her closely.

Two soldiers, one colored and one white, parked the car in the yard. They got out, leaving the motor running and their car doors open, as though they were planning to make a quick getaway. As they walked up to the porch, the colored soldier was carrying some papers in his hand. The white soldier remained silent while the colored soldier did most of the talking.

"Good evening folks," the colored soldier said. "We're here to speak to Mr. and Mrs. Boggs."

"I'm Mr. Boggs," Mr. Henry answered hesitantly. "And, this is my wife, Emma."

"Are you here with news about my son, Sam?" Mrs. Emma asked.

"I'm sorry to say, ma'am," the colored soldier responded, "but… yes, I am."

"Is he hurt badly?" Mrs. Boggs inquired. "When will they be sending him home?"

"I wish the news was that good, ma'am," the colored soldier said, "but…"

"Oh my God!" Mrs. Boggs screamed. "Not my beloved Sam!"

"Is he dead?" Mr. Henry asked.

"Yes, sir," the white soldier answered.

“He was killed in action and you have our deepest condolences,” the colored soldier added.

When the colored soldier gave the papers he was carrying to Mr. Henry, Mrs. Emma fainted and almost fell off the porch before Cleo caught her. Sarah and Lilly helped Cleo carry Mrs. Emma into the house to lay her on her bed. Sarah and Lilly held her hands as she hysterically wept.

Sarah clearly empathized with the pain that Mrs. Emma was feeling because she had once received the same bad news when she lost her son, John, to another war.

As the stoic-faced soldiers got back in their car and drove away, Belinda jumped off the porch and was screaming. She ran behind their car and picked up some rocks, throwing them at the moving car. She did not stop until the car was out of her sight. She then ran deep into the woods. Dog, trailing behind her, howled as if he sensed that his master was dead.

Stunned by the horrific news of Sam’s death, Mr. Henry and Iris were the only two left standing, motionless, on the porch.

Mr. Henry crumbled the papers that he was holding with one hand. He continued to mumble, “My son is dead! My son is dead!”

Iris grasped her stomach tightly. She did not want to lose the only thing she had left of her darling Sam. But, for some reason, she could not bring herself to cry. All Iris felt was contempt for Sam. At that moment, she hated him for dying and leaving her to raise their baby alone.

Mr. Henry then walked over to Iris and whispered, “I know how much Sam loved you and wanted you to become his wife. As far as we are concerned, you’ll always be a member of this family. Don’t you worry; we’ll get through this together. When my grandbaby is born, Emma and I are going to keep the promise we made. We want you to still see to it that your dream of becoming a school teacher comes true.”

"Mr. Henry, you know that I loved Sam," Iris said softly.

"Without a doubt," Mr. Henry replied.

"Then, why am I not crying?" Iris asked in a somber voice.

"Your tears will come when you're ready," Mr. Henry assured. "Take care of that baby. That's all we have left of our Sam."

With the crumbled papers still in his fist, Mr. Henry went into the deep woods in search of Belinda and Dog.

Iris followed Mr. Boggs down the steps and into the middle of the yard before allowing him to go on alone. She stopped and watched as he disappeared amongst the tall trees.

Of all the times Iris had visited the Boggses, it was the first time she ever heard the sound of an airplane flying overhead. She looked up into the clear blue sky and saw an airplane moving slowly across it. The sound was so sad and lonesome to her ears. As the plane flew out of sight, Iris finally started to cry.

"Sam, I love you!" Iris cried aloud. "I'll always love you. As long as I live, I'll never love another man. Please forgive me for the evil thoughts I had about you. I know you didn't mean to leave me all alone and pregnant. It's not your fault that you died fighting for a country where us colored folks don't even have the same rights as the white folks."

The sight of Mr. Henry, walking back towards the house with Belinda, distracted Iris from her thoughts. He had given Belinda the white rag, which he used as a handkerchief, so she could wipe her teary eyes. When Belinda saw Iris, she ran and hugged her. They threw their arms tightly around each other and began to wail.

"You two girls have to stop crying," Mr. Henry pleaded. "I got a favor to ask."

“What is it, Daddy?” Belinda inquired.

“Me, you, and Iris got to be strong for Emma,” Mr. Henry said. “She’s a very frail woman. I don’t know if she can handle losing Sam. She had one nervous breakdown when she had a miscarriage before you and Sam was born. I don’t know if she can recover from losing another child.”

“I didn’t know Mama had a baby before me and Sam,” Belinda said, surprised.

“Your mama use to be a maid for my family. We were planning to run away and go up North to get married. Emma confided in Nelly, our other maid who had raised my twin brother, Jim, and me since we were babies, about our plans. Out of jealousy, Nelly told my mama. My mama put her hands on Emma’s stomach and said, ‘If my son marries you, nigger, every child you conceive will die.’” Mr. Boggs continued, “When Emma lost our first child, she began to believe in Mama’s curse. I’m sure she will believe the curse has begun to haunt her again! You see... that’s why I need you girls to help me take care of her.”

“You can count on me, Daddy,” Belinda responded.

“Me too,” Iris added.

“Iris, are you still going to live with us?” Belinda asked.

“Of course she is,” Mr. Henry interrupted. “We’re going to continue with our plans. By the time the baby is born, Emma will be her old self again! Now, let’s go in the house and check on her now! She needs us!”

They then went into the house and joined Sarah and Lilly, who remained at the Boggses’ until late in the evening. They tried their best to console Iris, Emma, Henry, and Belinda. But, it was getting very late and Lilly had to go to work early the following morning.

Cleo, who had fled from Mrs. Emma's room as soon as he had laid her on her bed, was sitting in his car waiting to drive Sarah and Lilly back home. His arms were tightly clenched across his chest and he was rocking back and forth like a sleepy child. That was one of the things he often did when he was stressed by a problem or he felt something was beyond his control.

Lilly and Sarah knew if they did not get Cleo home soon, he would flee back into the woods like he did on the day of his brother, John's, funeral. He disappeared for days before finally returning home carrying five dead squirrels in a burlap sack.

Before leaving the Boggses' house, Sarah and Lilly stored all of the food inside the icebox and poured out the unfrozen ice cream, from the churn, into the yard. Neither of them had an appetite after the news of Sam's death.

* * * * *

After that tragic day, Lilly and Sarah often visited Iris and the Boggses. Both families were impatiently waiting for Sam's body to be shipped back to the United States for burial. But, their wait would be two long, agonizing months.

A black hearse, driven by two white soldiers, arrived at the Boggses' house. Inside the hearse was Sam's body. Another car, carrying four colored soldiers, also trailed closely behind the hearse.

The four colored soldiers carried Sam's casket, draped with an American flag, into the house. The white soldiers waited outside and did not drive away until Sam's body was safely inside.

The colored soldiers placed Sam's casket against the wall of the narrow hallway. Because most colored people lived in poverty and did not have a nearby mortuary that was willing to serve them at their establishments—many families had to view their deceased within the confines of their homes. Colored families were lucky if the corpses of their loved ones were even embalmed. Only white families enjoyed that humane privilege. Crosstown was not yet ready for a dead colored person to rest amongst their deceased whites—not even if it was a soldier who had fought and died protecting their country. The few white mortuaries that allowed coloreds were so far away that most poor families could not afford, neither had reliable transportation, to travel to them.

Two of the four colored soldiers, dressed in full military attire, left with the two white soldiers. The other two colored soldiers remained behind in order to guard Sam's body. They needed to make sure that his sealed casket was not opened nor looked inside of. They were assigned with the task of guarding Sam's body until he was buried the following day.

Throughout the night, while the Boggses and Iris mourned and kept vigil over Sam's casket, the two soldiers took turns standing at attention. They did not eat any food or drink any water. Neither did they speak to anyone.

At noon the next day, Lilly and Sarah arrived at the Boggses to attend Sam's graveside burial. Mr. Henry was wearing a dusty black suit and Belinda had on a faded black dress. Iris was wearing the new black dress that Sarah had recently bought her from the mercantile store.

They were all ready for the funeral, except for Mrs. Emma. She was just walking around aimlessly, wearing a black slip, and talking incoherently to herself. She had been manifesting this odd behavior ever since she had learned of Sam's death. With Lilly and Sarah's help, Mr. Henry finally got Mrs. Emma dressed and out of the house.

The hearse returned and Sam's body was placed in the back. It slowly drove the short distance to the Boggses' family cemetery.

Mr. Henry had hired an old colored man and his son to dig Sam's grave and place mismatched chairs, from the house, for everyone to sit in. Three of the soldiers, carrying their rifles, walked alongside the hearse so that the Boggses and Iris could ride inside. Sarah and Lilly walked next to the soldiers, followed closely by Dog.

As the Boggses and Jacksons took their seats, Sam's casket was taken out of the hearse and placed in front of his gravesite.

"Are there any other family members coming?" a soldier asked.

"Just us," Mr. Henry said tearfully.

"I'm a chaplain," a soldier said. "Would you like me to recite Psalms 23?"

"It would make me very happy," Mr. Henry replied.

"What about you, Mrs. Boggs?" the chaplain asked.

"She's not well," Mr. Henry answered.

"Then, I'll begin," the chaplain said.

After the chaplain's recitation, the soldiers raised their rifles and fired a Three-Volley Salute into the air. Dog, startled by the sound of the rifles, dashed into the woods.

Before Sam's body was finally lowered into the ground—to be covered by the old man and his son who were standing in wait—two soldiers, one white and one colored, carefully removed and folded the American flag that draped his casket. They placed it in Mrs. Boggs' lap and presented a Purple Heart to Mr. Boggs.

Iris had to bite her tongue to restrain herself from shouting, "That flag and Purple Heart belong to me and Sam's unborn child." But, she remained silent because, regrettably, she was not his wife.

Mr. Henry, Emma, Belinda, and Iris returned to the hearse and were driven back to their house while Sarah and Lilly walked.

Sarah and Lilly left shortly after the soldiers departed the Boggses' house. Belinda and Iris then helped Mr. Henry undress Mrs. Emma and put her to bed. Mrs. Emma had fallen into an even deeper depression and was still mumbling to herself.

Iris felt so lonely without Sam. It was strange being in his parents' home, knowing that he would never be there again. She missed Sarah and Lilly, but was determined to adhere to her plan of letting Mr. Henry and Mrs. Emma raise her child while she attended college.

Now, more than ever, Iris would need an education and a well-paying job to raise and care for her child, especially as a single parent.

The night of Sam's funeral and every lonely night thereafter, Iris would reread the last letter she received from him before his untimely death.

My Darling Iris,

It is so lonely over here in this Godforsaken place. I'm dreaming of the time when I'm back at home with you and my baby. Daddy wants the baby to be a boy so he can continue the Boggs name.

However, I wouldn't mind having another beautiful Iris in the family. Whether our baby is a boy or a girl, I'm happy that the woman I love is carrying it.

Your love, my unborn child, and my family are the only things that keep me from losing my mind when I'm out here hiding in foxholes filled with rainwater.

Don't worry about our future or me, my darling, because everything will turn out fine. Never doubt, for one moment, that I love you.

When these miserable days have long since passed and I'm back home, we will again lie near the sandy banks of the creek on our favorite blanket, let Dog lick our faces, make passionate love, and have more babies. This will be our destiny until we are either too old or the creek runs dry!

With all my love,

Sam

CHAPTER 14

Every morning since Sam's funeral, Mrs. Emma would get out of bed, put on her robe, and visit his grave. She would stay there for hours until Mr. Henry would force her to come back to the house. Most days she could barely eat, sleep, or talk. Everyone feared that her depression would cause her to go insane or to commit suicide.

Mr. Henry was hoping that the birth of their grandchild would help her snap out of it. If Mrs. Emma's mental health did not improve, he would have to leave their old homestead and take her to Detroit where her sisters, Beatrice and Mary, could help him find her some professional counseling. They claimed that Detroit had doctors that specialized in Mrs. Emma's condition.

In the evenings, Iris and Belinda would search in the woods for Dog, but they could never find him. Eventually, when they had all but given up, Dog made his way to Sam's grave and would howl into the wee hours of the morning. Dog refused to eat the food or drink the water that Mr. Henry would leave for him. Like Mrs. Emma—Dog just wanted to die, which he eventually did.

Late one night, Iris and Belinda heard Mr. Henry pleading with Mrs. Emma. Mr. Henry was trying to keep Mrs. Emma from banging her head against their iron bedpost. A small stream of blood was trickling down Mrs. Emma's forehead. Sam's death had nearly driven her insane. Iris and Belinda helped Mr. Henry hold her down until she was too exhausted and eventually fell asleep.

Early that next morning, Mr. Henry came into Iris and Belinda's bedroom to inform them that he was going to ask Sarah if she would stay with them while he took Mrs. Emma to see a specialist in Detroit. He hated to awaken the very tired girls, especially after their ordeal with Mrs. Emma the night before, but he wanted to let them know that he was leaving the house for a few hours and needed them to care for her until he returned.

"What's wrong, Daddy?" Belinda asked, sitting up in bed. "Is Mama all right?"

"She's still asleep," Mr. Henry answered. "Iris, do you think your grandmother would come down here and stay with you and Belinda while Emma and I take a short trip to Detroit?"

"Maybe… if you ask her," Iris responded, rubbing her eyes, which were heavy from exhaustion.

"Why are you taking Mama to Detroit?" Belinda asked.

"I want your Mama to see a doctor that specializes in her kind of problem. I'm sure she'll recover quickly and we'll be home before our grandbaby is born."

"Don't worry, Daddy," Belinda said. "If Miss Sarah can't come, Iris and I can take care of ourselves until you and Mama get back."

"I can't take the chance of leaving two teen-age girls, one pregnant, alone down here in these woods, for days, with only lamplights and candles," Mr. Henry responded. "God only knows what kind of wild animals and unsavory people that might try to harm y'all! How would y'all get food or firewood for the stove? What if you or Iris gets sick? Or worse, what if the baby comes early?"

"I didn't think about that," Belinda reflected.

"Well, I did," Mr. Henry, said. "That's why I'm going to ask Sarah to come down here."

"Mr. Henry, please convince Mama to come and stay with us," Iris pleaded.

"I'm going to do my best," Mr. Henry responded. "Now you girls get out of bed and cook you some breakfast. If Emma wakes up before I get back, try to get her to eat something."

"Yes, sir," Belinda responded.

Mr. Henry then drove immediately to Sarah's house.

When she heard the knock on her front door, Sarah went to see who it was. Realizing that it was Mr. Henry, she opened the door and invited him to come inside.

"Is Iris in labor?" Sarah nervously asked.

"Iris is fine and so is Belinda. It's my wife who's sick. She's just about lost her mind ever since Sam died. I got to get her some help before it's too late!"

"I'm so sorry, Henry," Sarah said with regret in her voice. "It's not easy losing a child."

"Thanks for understanding, Sarah. I'm leaving for Detroit tomorrow and I'm taking Emma with me to see a doctor."

"What about Iris and Belinda? Who'll be there to watch them? What if the baby comes before y'all get home?"

"That's the reason I'm here. I want to ask for your help."

"Anything I can do to help, I will."

"Would you please come down to our house and stay with the girls until we return? If the baby comes before we get back, you'll know what to do… won't you?"

"I sure would," Sarah said boastfully. "I darn near brought Iris into this world all by myself."

"Then can I count on you?"

"Henry, it's a bad time for me to be leaving the house right now. My son, Cleo, is in a delicate situation where he may end up in a lot of trouble and need my help. But, I can't let those two girls stay alone in those woods to be eaten by wolves, or mountain lions, or heaven knows what else! And, I'm not going to let my great grandbaby be born without me around! I'll just pray that you and Emma come back soon."

Sarah was hesitant to leave her house because Cleo had begun to hang around a nefarious neighborhood called Colored Alley. He had also befriended some well-known criminals and thugs. Sarah felt that he was associating with men and women that could potentially get him into some serious trouble. Cleo had become infatuated with Crosstown's infamous prostitute, the beautiful Miss Wilma Lee. Sarah was positive that if Cleo continued to associate with the likes of Wilma Lee that he would either catch an incurable disease, go to prison for killing someone, or be murdered himself.

As long as Sarah could remember, Cleo had never had a girlfriend. She, along with many others in Crosstown, had begun to suspect that Cleo, a man in his late thirties, must be queer.

An oblivious Cleo had no idea that a few of the colored men in town had hired Miss Wilma Lee to seduce and sleep with him. Their instructions were clear; they wanted to know if he was a homosexual. Miss Wilma Lee was asked to report back to them after she had some proof that either proved or disproved their theory.

Miss Wilma Lee eventually upheld her part of the deal, for which she was paid. She even kept the pair of Cleo's dirty and holey underwear that he was wearing as a trophy of her deceitful work. She told the men that Cleo was sexually inexperienced, but with her guidance, he quickly learned. She also told them that he was certainly not a homosexual.

As far as Wilma Lee was concerned, that one and only sexual encounter would be her last. But, Cleo had other plans. He was infatuated with her and had even begun to stalk her. Even though she was the town's prostitute, Cleo wanted to marry her and make her into a decent woman. However, what Cleo did not fully understand was that Miss Wilma Lee could never be just one man's woman.

If Cleo ever faced the truth, Sarah feared that the humiliation would be too much for him to handle. With his explosive temper, she felt that he might fly into one of his rages and kill Miss Wilma Lee—like he had previously tried to do to a man that he once caught stealing a raccoon from one of his traps. If it had not been for the two other trappers, restraining Cleo and allowing the man to flee, he most certainly would have killed him. Sarah knew that if Cleo would kill over a raccoon, he definitely would kill over being betrayed by a woman that he loved.

* * * * *

The day after Mr. Boggs' visit, Sarah went to care for Iris and Belinda. Mr. Henry had already packed his and Mrs. Emma's suitcases by the time she arrived. They were scheduled to leave on the midnight train to Detroit.

Sarah, Belinda, and Iris spent most of their days relaxing around the house after the Boggses left. Although Sarah would often walk down to the creek to fish, Belinda and Iris rarely left the house.

One day after an early supper, Sarah left Belinda and Iris at home while she went fishing. Belinda was washing the dishes while Iris was sitting at the kitchen table.

Suddenly, Iris began to experience stomach pains. She joked that it was the collard greens that Belinda had cooked for supper.

They both laughed until water began to flow uncontrollably from underneath Iris' dress. Belinda almost fainted at the sight of the puddle of water on the floor.

"What's wrong with you?" Belinda screamed.

"I don't know!" Iris hollered.

"Are you having the baby?"

"I don't know! I must be! Go get Mama and tell her to come quick!"

Belinda threw the plate that she was washing back into the dishpan before running to get Sarah.

By the time Sarah and Belinda returned to the house, Iris was on the kitchen floor and had given birth to a beautiful baby girl. She had already named her Samantha Boggs.

All Sarah had to do was cut the umbilical cord and take the crying baby out of Iris' exhausted grip. Belinda helped Iris get cleaned up and into bed.

For the next month, Sarah continued to live at the Boggses' home. She was helping Iris and Belinda take care of baby Samantha. However, they were all waiting to receive some type of update from Mr. and Mrs. Boggs about when they expected to return from Detroit.

Belinda finally got word, from her father, that the specialist said that it would be a long time before her mother would be well enough to come home. Mrs. Emma had sunken into an even deeper melancholic state. Mr. Henry informed Belinda that the doctor felt that Mrs. Emma might never be able to live a normal life if she did not overcome her malaise. Mr. Henry requested that Belinda secure their house, pack everything that she could fit on a train, and travel to Detroit to help him care for her mother.

After learning about the news of Mrs. Emma's condition, there was nothing left for Iris to do—but to swallow her pride. She and Samantha would now have to return home to live with Sarah and Lilly. The embarrassed and defeated Iris would have to abandon her plans of attending college at Tuskegee Institute while Mr. Henry and Mrs. Emma cared for Samantha. Her only choice was to work at Cleo's Place, raise her daughter, and face the fact that she had become another statistic among the many other colored girls in Crosstown who, because of BROKEN PROMISES, had failed to accomplish their dreams.

The day Belinda's train was scheduled to leave, she and Iris said their goodbyes. They embraced and promised to always remain best friends. Belinda then traveled up North while Iris and Samantha remained down South.

Iris was secretly envious of Belinda. She was jealous of the realization that Belinda, although under dire circumstances, had escaped Crosstown and that she, a newly single mother, was unable to do the same.

The town's gossipers were frivolously spreading rumors about how Iris had birthed a little white baby out of wedlock. They were also making fun of Cleo for dating the town's whore. The whispers and rumors sent Sarah into a tailspin. For the first time in her life, Sarah felt as though she was no better than the other "niggers" of Crosstown.

Due to her extreme disappointment in Iris, sometimes Sarah would stay in bed all day. She would only get out of it to use the chamber pot. Sarah had even begun to have a foul body odor. She reeked of urine because she was not bathing or changing her nightgown.

During this phase, Iris would cook and bring Sarah's meals to her bedside. Lilly was unable to assist her due to being overworked at the café and usually going directly to sleep when she got home.

Iris felt trapped, deserted, lonely, and old beyond her years. She was not only frustrated at Sarah's unresponsiveness, but also that she had not heard from Belinda since she left for Detroit. To make matters worse, Samantha was colicky. Sometimes Iris would find herself thinking about Sam and hating him for dying. If Sarah was trying to punish her for being a disappointment, she was doing a damn good job!

CHAPTER 15

Iris awoke to the sound of pots and pans being moved around in the kitchen. Before getting out of bed to investigate, she checked to see if Lilly and Samantha were still asleep. Iris was surprised to find Sarah groomed and wearing a clean dress. She was stirring a pot of grits and frying a slab of ham.

When Sarah realized that Iris was watching her, she stopped stirring the grits and began to tell Iris about the epiphany she had had the night before.

"Iris, last night while I was in my bed, I suddenly came to the conclusion that I've been behaving selfishly. Perhaps, I've been trying to force my children, and even you, to live the life that I always wanted for myself. I now realize that I was wrong and I'm truly sorry."

"You don't have to apologize," Iris responded. "I want Samantha to succeed beyond my dreams, too."

"Don't make the same mistakes that I did. And, if you want, I'll raise Samantha and you can still go to college."

"Thanks, Mama. But, I'm going to keep the promise that I made to you and to Lilly… and to myself. I promised that if something ever happened to the plans that Sam and I made with the Boggs or if your prediction came true, that I would stay home, get a job at the café, and raise my child myself."

"Are you sure, Iris?"

"I'm sure, Mama. But, I love you for asking."

"If you change your mind, just let me know."

"I will, Mama."

Iris and Sarah stopped talking when Cleo unexpectedly walked into the kitchen. He had let himself inside the house more quietly than usual. Cleo greeted them and then sat at the table. He told Iris and Sarah that he had come to see if Lilly needed a ride to work.

"Good morning, Son," Sarah said. "Would you like some breakfast?"

"Sure, Mama," Cleo responded.

As Cleo ate his breakfast, Sarah and Iris sat next to him drinking coffee. Lilly soon joined them in the kitchen and fixed her a bowl of grits.

"Mama, you remember when I told you about a surprise announcement that I would soon make?" Cleo asked.

"I hope it's about you finding a lot of money buried in those backwoods," Lilly joked.

"Stop teasing your brother and let him talk," Sarah demanded.

"Mama," Cleo began nervously, "I'm going to ask Wilma Lee to marry me."

"Have you lost your mind?" Sarah asked. "Don't you know that woman has slept with just about every colored man and every white man in Crosstown?"

"That was in her past!" Cleo shouted. "She's a changed woman!"

"If she marries you," Sarah responded, "it's because she wants your money and to inherit Cleo's Place… the café that I helped you buy so you'd have something to fall back on when I die!"

"Mama, you used the money that I saved," Cleo said. "That place is mine!"

“That’s true; it was your money,” Sarah lamented. “But that doesn’t change the fact that Wilma Lee is a skinny, yellowtail harlot, gold-digger.”

“No, she’s not!” Cleo exploded. “Wilma Lee loves me!”

Sensing that the dispute was about to take a turn for the worse, Iris immediately left the kitchen and went to check on Samantha. She was all too familiar with the angry side of the gentle giant that she called Uncle Cleo. Iris had heard stories about how his temper could be explosively fatal if he were pushed beyond his breaking point. Iris sat in Sarah’s rocking chair, holding Samantha in her arms, and listened to their quarrelling.

“Cleo,” Lilly began, “the only reason Wilma Lee slept with you was because she was paid to make a fool of you! It’s the talk of the town. Everyone knows it was a scam, but you!”

“You’re lying!” Cleo screamed.

“It’s true,” Lilly said calmly. “We just didn’t want to hurt you. We were hoping that your lust for Wilma Lee would blow over by now.”

“I don’t want that nasty bitch to be a part of this family,” Sarah shouted, “so stop being a fool… Fool!”

“Don’t call me a fool, Mama!” Cleo shouted back. “I’m tired of you calling me a fool! I’m not a child or a fool! When I leave here, I’m going straight to Wilma’s house and ask her to marry me! There’s nothing you or Lilly can do to stop me!”

“I can promise you this Cleo, if you marry that woman, I won’t continue to work at the café,” Lilly said. “I won’t let Wilma Lee be my boss!”

“You don’t have to work for me,” Cleo retorted. “Wilma can run the café from now on!”

"Leave my house, now!" Sarah shouted. "If you don't forget your foolish ideas about marrying that slut, don't ever come back!"

"I won't!" Cleo exclaimed.

"Oh you'll be back," Sarah said sarcastically, "because I feel a cold chill...."

"To Hell with your fortune telling, Mama!" Cleo interrupted.

Cleo then jumped up from the table, spilling his coffee. He slung a chair against the wall before storming out of the kitchen, passing by Iris and Samantha without saying a word. Before rushing out the front door, he punched a hole into the wall.

Later on that evening, Cleo burst back into the house holding a shotgun. There was blood splattered on his clothes and face. He rushed by Iris, who was reading one of Sarah's romance novels, and went into the kitchen where Sarah and Lilly were chatting and preparing supper.

As soon as Cleo was in the kitchen, Iris grabbed Samantha and ran outside. She fled to the backyard and hid behind the old chinaberry tree.

Lilly could sense something was terribly wrong by Sarah's abrupt silence. Keeping her eyes fixated on Cleo, Sarah stopped grating sweet potatoes and slowly rose from her chair. Lilly, who was snapping string beans, was petrified. Although she wanted to run, she was glued to her seat. All Lilly could do was pray that Iris and Samantha were safely out of the house. Judging by the insane look on Cleo's face, Lilly was sure they were all going to die.

"Son, don't do something you'll regret," Sarah said calmly. "Give me the shotgun."

Cleo began to cry like a frightened child. He then hesitantly handed Sarah the shotgun. Sarah carefully took the gun away from Cleo's grasp and stood it against the wall. Cleo, unable to stay still, continued to cry as he paced back and forth. Mucus was dripping from his nose and into his mouth as he fidgeted with his hands.

"Son, what have you done?" Sarah asked. "Please stop crying and tell me so I can help you."

"You and Lilly was right," Cleo cried.

"What were we right about?" Sarah asked.

"Wilma Lee," Cleo answered.

"Cleo, what happened?" Lilly asked frantically.

"I… I killed her!" Cleo stuttered.

"Who did you kill?" Sarah asked.

"Wilma Lee," Cleo responded.

"Please tell me that you're joking," Sarah stated.

"Mama, I'm not joking," Cleo said. "She's dead!"

"Why did you kill her?" Lilly asked, stunned.

"I went over to her house to ask her to marry me. Her front door was unlocked and I walked right in. She was on top of her bed with that old white man, David Poole. Mama… they were naked!"

"That cracker?" Sarah asked. "The one whose wife and him use to buy catfish from you?"

"Yes, ma'am," Cleo answered.

"Why didn't you just leave?" Lilly inquired.

"I was… until she called me a fool," Cleo cried. "She told me to get out of her house. Something just exploded inside me! I went to my car and got my shotgun. I then ran back inside to kill them both. But, when Mr. Poole saw me, he jumped out of the window butt naked. Wilma was so scared that she just lay there screaming, 'Please don't kill me! Please don't kill me!' But, I just started beating her over her head with my shotgun until I realized she was dead."

"Lilly," Sarah said breathlessly, "we got to get Cleo out of Crosstown right away before anyone finds Wilma's body. Mr. James isn't alive to help me anymore. If he were still living, he would get Cleo out of this mess. So, we will have to do it by ourselves." Sarah paused before continuing, "Lilly, I'll be damn if I'm going to let my son go to prison. You know your brother couldn't survive being trapped in a prison cell, twiddling his thumbs until he goes mad, all because he killed a whore. My Cleo was born to roam free, not to be locked up in a cage like a wild animal!"

"What if Mr. Poole went to Sheriff Goodson's office and reported Cleo?" Lilly asked. "The deputies could already be at Wilma's house. They might be on their way to our house to arrest Cleo now!"

"If David Poole told Sheriff Goodson, he and his vigilantes would already be here handcuffing Cleo," Sarah retorted angrily. "That married redneck won't tell anybody that he was sleeping with a colored hooker! So, he certainly wouldn't have the nerve to name her killer." Sarah then said, "Cleo… stop fidgeting! I want you to go out to the car, lay down in the back seat, and wait for me and Lilly."

"Mama," Cleo asked, "what're you going to do?"

"Lilly and I are going to drive you as far back into the deep woods as we possibly can. You need to get lost in the wilderness until this mess blows over."

"Yes, ma'am." Cleo said obediently.

"Lilly, go and get Iris," Sarah said. "She's hiding behind the chinaberry tree with Samantha."

"How do you know where she's hiding?" Lilly asked.

"It's the same place she used to hide when she was a little girl," Sarah answered.

When Iris and Samantha were back safely inside the house, Sarah told her not to open the door for anyone. Sarah also instructed Iris that if anyone asked her if she had seen Cleo to say no.

Sarah and Lilly then drove Cleo back to the café where they helped him pack some of his belongings into a large duffel bag. Afterwards, they drove him as far as they could into the deep woods. As they drove, everyone was silent except for Cleo, who was sobbing loudly in the backseat.

It was getting very late into the evening and Lilly was afraid to drive any farther down the isolated trails. She could not take the chance that they would get lost and not find their way back home.

"Mama, I believe this is as far as I should drive this old Ford," Lilly said. "It's getting late and soon we won't be able to follow the tracks back out."

"Cleo, can you make it safely from here?" Sarah asked.

"Yes, ma'am," Cleo responded.

Cleo, with his duffel bag strapped across his shoulder, exited the car and so did Sarah and Lilly. They both held Cleo's hand as they stood by the edge of the isolated road. It was the first time since John's funeral that Lilly and Cleo had seen their mother disconsolate. Sarah then pulled Cleo close and hugged him.

"Son, I love you," Sarah said with tears streaming down her face. "Please take care of yourself."

"I will, Mama," Cleo sobbed. "I promise you that somehow or someway… I'll let you know that I'm still alive and well."

"My sweet baby…" Sarah stuttered. "If you can't, I'll understand."

"Take care of yourself," Lilly said. "I love you, Cleo."

"I know you do," Cleo responded. "That's why I want Cleo's Place to be yours." Looking at Sarah, he continued, "Mama, the rest of my money is hidden in the bottom of that old trunk where I keep all of my hunting and fishing gear. It's yours now. Tell Iris and Samantha that I said goodbye and I'm sorry for scaring them."

Sarah and Lilly were crying as they watched Cleo hurry away into the dark woods, leaving them standing by their car. He continued on foot until he disappeared into the dense undergrowth.

It was another sad day for the Jackson family. Sarah and Lilly hesitated before getting back into their car and driving home.

* * * * *

By the time Miss Wilma Lee's body was discovered, Cleo had long since vanished. Although there were rumblings and whispers about his whereabouts, no one in Crosstown could ever claim that they physically saw him again.

Wilma Lee had so many different men, in and out of her life, that it could have been any one of them, or their wives, who wanted her dead. Sarah was certain that no white man would come forward and confess that he was cheating with a colored woman. Furthermore, a white man would never ruin his reputation in order to bring a colored man to justice for killing a woman infamously known as the town's prostitute. Besides, every woman in Crosstown was glad to be rid of the beautiful Wilma Lee. Most of them felt that she had it coming and that she had gotten exactly what she deserved.

Over the next several years, Sarah would sometimes open her back-door to find freshly killed rabbits, squirrels, opossums, raccoons, or catfish on her porch. They would be neatly wrapped in a burlap sack. She knew it was Cleo's way of giving her a sign that he was still alive.

As the years slowly passed, the burlap sacks of goodies eventually stopped coming. Sarah knew, in her heart, that Cleo would never abandon her unless it was beyond his immediate control. She suspected that he must be dead. Nevertheless, she could not bring herself to give up hope that one day he would reappear.

Sarah silently mourned her beloved Cleo's life and possible death—just as Mr. Parker James had once done when he secretly mourned the death of their other son, John.

Sarah smiled at the thought of Cleo roaming free in the woods, a place he always loved and considered his second home. She mumbled under her breath, "If he's dead, at least he died a free man! Roam free… my sweet, sweet Cleo!"

CHAPTER 16

Samantha was now twelve years old. She had just begun to menstruate. Iris felt that since Samantha had started her menstrual cycle that it was time to officially talk to her about the birds and the bees. When they finally sat down for their mother-daughter talk, Samantha already knew more about sex than Iris ever did when she was her age. However, Iris begged her to pledge that she would remain a virgin until she was at least twenty-one years old. Samantha embarrassingly assured her that she would.

At thirteen years old, Samantha skipped from the eighth to the tenth grade due to being highly intelligent and gifted. The change was not an easy transition, for she was much younger and shorter than her classmates. Many of the older girls did not befriend her and often teased her about being fair-skinned. They would also repeat the gossip, which they had heard from their mothers, about her being a bastard child because her parents were not married when she was conceived.

Although extremely smart, Samantha was becoming discontent with school. She was slowly transforming into an ostracized loner, feeling as though neither her peers nor family understood her. There were many days that she would come home from school and just cry herself to sleep. Iris would look at Samantha, who strongly resembled her grandfather, Mr. Henry, asleep with her long, straight hair covering the pillow and a frown upon her beautiful face. Iris wished that she could erase all of her daughter's troubles, but she did not know how.

All Samantha knew about her father was that his name was Samuel Boggs and that he was a soldier when he was killed in action. The only picture she had of him was a very small photo, taken during his basic training, which Iris had given to her. When she was really depressed, Samantha would sleep with Sam's picture underneath her pillow. Iris' heart ached for her daughter. Like mother, like daughter—both knew the pain of not having a father around to protect them. But the reasons for their absentee fathers were substantially different. Samantha's father was an honorable man who loved and wanted to marry her mother. Contrastingly, Iris' father was a child molester that fled town to avoid prosecution.

When Samantha was not crying herself to sleep, she could always find comfort in the waiting, loving arms of her great-grandmother, Sarah. Every time she walked through the door, Sarah would have freshly-baked cookies, cakes, or pies prepared for her. All Samantha wanted to do was play Gin Rummy with her great-grandmother and eat until it was bedtime.

For Sarah, Samantha was like having her beloved daughter, Rose, back home. Iris loved witnessing the close relationship that Sarah and Samantha shared. Nonetheless, Samantha was becoming heavier and more depressed as the days passed. Even her love for Sarah was beginning to do little, if any, to curb her downward spiral. During this time, Iris simply wanted Samantha to complete high school and go to college. She had faith that leaving Crosstown would give Samantha an opportunity to start anew and acquire some better friends.

At fifteen years old, Samantha was Valedictorian of her class. She was also the youngest student to ever graduate from Mary Hines Johnson and the second youngest student to ever receive a full scholarship to the famous, and integrated, Auburn University.

The Jackson's—Sarah, Lilly, and Iris—held their heads high as they sat in the front row of the auditorium during Samantha's high-school graduation. It was music to their ears to hear her name being called and her achievements being read aloud by the principal, Mr. George Robert Moore. When it was time for the obese Samantha to receive her diploma, she proudly rose from her seat and wobbled across the stage.

Iris could hear giggling coming from the audience. Samantha must have also heard the heckling because she quickly accepted her diploma and scholarship before leaving via a side door. When Sarah,

Lilly, and Iris got to the car, Samantha was already sitting in the back seat. On their ride home, they attempted to describe how proud they were of Samantha, but she was not in the mood to listen.

They arrived home just in time to find Mr. Jack Jones, who had a large white envelope in his hand, preparing to leave their porch. He greeted Sarah and Lilly and then gave the envelop to Iris. While everyone else went inside to prepare for supper, Iris sat in the swing to review the contents of the envelope.

On the front were the words "From Belinda to Iris." Inside the envelope was a deed to a property attached to a three-page letter. Iris was overjoyed to hear from Belinda, Sam's sister and her old best friend. Iris silently read the letter, her fingers tracing over each word, as she used only her feet to swing back and forth.

My Dearest Iris,

I can't believe it's been fifteen years since we've seen each other. Yesterday on my way to work at the sewing factory, I ran into Mr. Jack Jones. He was up here visiting his sister, Mrs. Cora Mae, and his nieces, Evelyn and Annie. Mrs. Cora Mae is living with Evelyn in the tenement across the street from Annie and me. It sure is a small world that I happen to live in the same neighborhood as them.

I'm giving this important envelope to Mr. Jack to give to you. I know I can trust him to see that you get it and he promised me that he would. It's been a long time coming, but thank you for naming my niece after my brother. In a few weeks, Mr. Jack will be coming back to Detroit to help Evelyn and Annie care for Mrs. Cora Mae. Our old teacher has unfortunately fallen ill and mellowed out since she taught us at her school.

Annie and Mrs. Cora Mae said to tell you hello. Annie also told me to tell you that she was wrong and very sorry for what she did to you those many years ago. I asked her what she did to you, but she refused to tell me. She only said that you would know exactly what she was talking about.

I also want to apologize to you, Iris. I'm sorry that I dropped out of your life when you were having such a difficult time, but life hasn't been too kind to me either. Mama is still alive and lives in an institution for the insane. Even though she no longer recognizes me, I still go to visit her every Sunday. She was never able to pull herself out of her rut and return to a normal life after Sam's death.

Five years after we moved to Detroit, Daddy died of a broken heart. He never got over learning that Mama would never be the same. Neither did he fully get over Sam's death. Daddy always said that before he died, he would make it back to Crosstown to finally get to meet his granddaughter, Samantha. But with Mama's condition, he sadly never got a chance.

Daddy's twin brother, Mr. Jim, begged me to let him pay for Daddy's body to be returned home and laid to rest next to Sam. Now, Mr. Jim wants me to call him Uncle Jim and to forgive him for how he treated my daddy and mama as well as me and Sam. He said that he has one foot in the grave and wanted me to pardon him so that he could go to heaven. It's amazing how getting old can change a person.

I should have come to visit you and Samantha when I brought Daddy's body home, but I was too bitter. For a long time, I blamed you for my family's problems. I'm much older and wiser now. I know that it was not your fault.

My main reason for writing this letter is that I want to do something special for you and my niece. With Daddy dead and Mama in an asylum, I don't plan to ever return to Crosstown, Georgia—at least not to live. I'm making Detroit my home. So, I want you and my niece to have our old homestead and all the land we own. Please take the attached deed and accept it as a gift from The Boggs family to you and Samantha. I know Daddy would have wanted you to have it.

Iris, I want you to build a home for you, Samantha, Lilly, and the sweet Miss Sarah on our old land.

My only wish is for you to tend to Sam and Daddy's graves, as I will not be there to do it. Also, just in case our time comes sooner than later, do save a plot for Mama and me.

Your sister,

Belinda

Iris joined the others, who were in the kitchen eating dinner. She gave Belinda's letter to Samantha and asked her to read it aloud to Sarah and Lilly.

Samantha was annoyed that she was chosen to read the letter. After reading it aloud, she gave it back to Iris before nonchalantly continuing to eat. Even the part about the land that she and Iris had inherited did not faze her. Samantha's cold demeanor even surprised Sarah and Lilly, who were ecstatic over the good news.

"Samantha," Iris asked, "after college, wouldn't you like to return to Crosstown as a teacher and to build a home on the land of your ancestors?"

"I don't think so," Samantha said, shrugging her shoulders. "Especially not in Crosstown, Georgia! As soon as I get my college degree, I want to move to a big city like New York or Chicago to teach. I will marry a rich man and if I don't want to work, my husband will take care of my children and me. I don't want to be poor all of my life. And, I don't want to grow old and gray like the three of you."

"Samantha, you're very young now," Lilly said disappointedly. "As you get older, you'll see things much differently. At least, I hope you will!"

"I don't think so," Samantha responded.

Although she did not verbalize it, Iris knew that most of Samantha's words were true. She was in her mid thirties, single, with prematurely graying hair. As Iris looked around at Sarah and Lilly, she realized that they too had grown much older and grayer. Sarah's hair was completely gray and Lilly's was salt and pepper.

For the first time, Iris faced the fact that she, Sarah, and Lilly had become three old women with nothing exciting in their lives, but work and family drama. Iris could not remember the last time that a man asked her out on a date or even gave her a second glance.

For over a decade, Iris had devoted all of her energy to raising Samantha. She felt as though Samantha was ungrateful and unappreciative of all that she had sacrificed for her.

Iris then walked out of the kitchen and went into the bedroom, where she looked into the mirror. She ran her fingers through her graying hair and glanced at the old-fashioned dress that she was wearing. As Iris continued to stare at her reflection, the reality of Samantha's bluntness hit her like a ton of bricks.

Sarah, Lilly, Iris—and even Samantha's—lives had become like weakened links in a long rusted chain. Would their entanglement hold strong or would it become so strained that it would finally break?

CHAPTER 17

After Samantha left for college, Lilly surprised everyone when she announced that she was taking a hiatus from working at the café to spend more time with Sarah. Iris decided that since Samantha was no longer living at home that she would take over Lilly's position. Although she would be working more hours than her prior schedule entailed, this new managerial position would give her a way to stay busy while saving some extra money. However, Lilly suggested that Iris hire someone to help her and she recommended her best and most trusted friend, Mrs. Rozell White.

Every weekend and most weeknights, the café was crowded with customers. Hence, it was making a lot of money. This was beneficial to Iris because Samantha was constantly writing home to request large sums of money for food, school supplies, and clothes.

Everything seemed to be going smoothly with the new changes at Cleo's Place. Iris and Rozell were getting along well. No drunken fistfights had erupted in months. But, Iris' life was just as dull as ever. However, that would all change when she met Marvin Brown, a man from Roanoke, Alabama.

One night, a skinny Marvin Brown walked into the café to eat soul food and listen to soul music. His plaid shirt, old blue jeans, and boots smelled of cottonseed oil due to him working in a cotton gin. His skin was smooth and jet-black. His hair was kinky and caked with lint from cotton debris and his two front teeth were missing. When he walked into the café, he was so tall that he had to stoop down to avoid bumping his head on the doorframe. Neither married nor single women, in Cleo's Place, cared how Marvin looked or smelled because he was the best dancer in the whole place. It became a challenge for them to see which one of them he would ask to dance.

One Saturday night, Marvin asked Iris to dance. She declined by using the excuse that she had never learned, which was true. Iris did not want to look foolish like Rozell had when she tried to jitterbug with Marvin; Rozell danced like she had two left feet.

Iris, however, believed that she could learn how to dance if Marvin, who was usually the last customer to leave the café, would stay and give her some private lessons. When Iris discussed her plan with Rozell, she asked Iris to see if Marvin would also teach her. Iris was happy to include Rozell in her dance lessons. Furthermore, this would ensure that she would not have to be alone with the flirtatious Marvin.

After Cleo's Place closed for the night, Iris washed the dirty dishes and shot glasses before clearing the empty beer bottles off the tables. Rozell swept the floor and emptied the ashtrays. The jukebox played another song as Marvin continued to sit at the bar. Rozell was giving Iris signals to remind her not to forget to ask Marvin about teaching them how to dance.

"Marvin, you sure got some great dance moves," Iris said.

"Thanks… I do have my stuff together," Marvin bragged.

"Who taught you how to dance so well?" Iris asked.

"My mama," Marvin answered, reminiscing. "She died when she was just forty years old. I didn't have a daddy at home so as a young boy, my mama would take me to those juke joints and shot houses every Saturday night. Man oh man… everybody was there eating chitterlings, drinking moonshine, and dancing late into the night. My mama would never leave me home alone, so I watched her and every other person in the place dance. I guess I just picked up their best moves. After working a long day, Mama would come home and help me practice my steps. Wow, she sure was one good dancer!"

"Sorry to hear about your Mama dying so young," Iris said sympathetically.

“Me, too,” Rozell agreed.

“Thanks,” Marvin responded.

“Marvin, do you have a girlfriend or wife?” Rozell asked.

“Neither one,” he answered.

“Marvin, would you like to teach me and Rozell a few of your dance steps?” Iris asked.

“I haven’t seen you dance,” Marvin chuckled. “I know Rozell has two left feet, but I’ll try.”

“Thanks for the encouragement,” Rozell pouted.

“Rozell, I was just teasing you,” Marvin said apologetically. “When do you ladies want to start those lessons?”

“Next Saturday after closing time,” Iris answered. “Will that be too late for you to stay up and then drive back to Roanoke?”

“I don’t work on Sundays,” Marvin responded. “So when I do get home, I’ll sleep all day. Would you like to start tonight?”

“No! No!” Iris answered. “We’ll be ready on next Saturday.”

“Besides, I got to get home to my husband tonight,” Rozell said.

“I guess I better get going, too,” Marvin said. “Do you ladies need a ride home?”

“I have my own car, but thanks anyway,” Rozell answered.

“Iris, what about you?” Marvin asked. “Do you need a ride home?”

“No thanks,” Iris responded. “Rozell will drive me.”

"Then, I guess I'll be going," Marvin said.

Marvin gladly jumped at the opportunity to teach Iris how to dance. It was obvious that he wanted to establish a bond between him and her, even if it meant having Rozell around.

For the next several Saturdays after the café closed, Marvin gave Iris and Rozell dance lessons into the wee hours of the morning. For the first time in years, Iris found herself laughing, having fun, and forgetting about her woes.

Nevertheless, unbeknownst to them, someone had begun to spread rumors that Rozell was working overtime because she was having an affair with a tall, ugly, skinny, colored man named Marvin Brown. The gossip soon reached Mr. Bob White, Rozell's peg-legged husband.

During the entire five years of their marriage, Rozell and Bob tried unsuccessfully to conceive a baby. Although many in town whispered that Rozell was barren, it was secretly Bob who was sterile. Bob never doubted Rozell's love for him, but he was afraid that Rozell was so desperate to become a mother that she may consider Marvin as a potential sperm donor. No way was Bob going to allow another man to impregnate his wife.

The next Saturday that Rozell worked late into the night, Bob grabbed his shotgun and rode his tractor to Cleo's Place. He was going to see if there was any truth to the town's gossip.

On that particular night, the music was blaring from the jukebox. Iris was standing at the bar, watching Rozell and Marvin practice their dance moves. They were focusing so intently on their steps that only Iris could see Bob standing in the doorway with his shotgun.

Iris screamed at the top of her voice, "Bob! What are you doing here?"

Her scream startled Bob, causing him to lose his balance and accidentally fire his shotgun into the ceiling. White dust from the sheetrock fell out of the large hole that the blast caused. The loud sound got Rozell and Marvin's undivided attention, abruptly causing them to stop doing the Camel Walk.

Marvin then dived head first out of the closest open window. Rozell fled out of the back door, hopped into her car, and sped away. They both left a frightened Iris hiding under the bar. She would have to face an angry Bob White by herself.

Iris found the courage to stand up and look at Bob, who was now sitting on a barstool. He had a toothless grin on his face. On the bar, directly in front of him, was a crumbled up ten-dollar bill that he had taken out of his pocket. Iris was so afraid that he was going to kill her that urine trickled down her legs.

"Did you see that jack rabbit jump out that window?" Bob asked, smiling. "You take this ten dollars and fix that hole in your ceiling. I'm going home to my wife. She should be there by now."

"Bob, please don't kill Rozell!" Iris pleaded. "She was just learning how to dance."

"Hell no… I love my wife too much to kill her," Bob responded. "Since I lost my leg, I haven't been a good husband to Rozell. But I can assure you that's all fixing to change just as soon as me and this here wobbly leg of mine get home."

Bob, using his shotgun as a crutch, limped outside. He got on his tractor and then rode away.

After Iris was sure that Bob was gone, she went outside to see if Marvin was just hiding somewhere or if he had really gotten into his white Cadillac and abandoned her, too.

Marvin's car was still parked on the side of the street, but he was nowhere in sight. Iris was about to go back inside of the café when she heard him calling her name.

"Iris!"

"Marvin, where are you?"

"Over here, behind the trees."

"He's gone! You can stop hiding now."

"Are you sure?"

"Yes! Let's go back in the café."

"Wait! I can't walk too fast! I lost one of my boots and cut my foot on a broken beer bottle!"

Marvin emerged from hiding behind some trees. In the moonlight, Iris could see leaves and small twigs embedded inside his kinky hair and clinging to his wrinkled clothes. He was wearing only one boot. A small stream of blood was trickling down the side of his face. Iris wanted to laugh at Marvin, but he looked too pathetic.

"Thank God that window you jumped through was open! You could've seriously injured yourself!"

"I had to! That crazy man had a shotgun! He was going to kill me!"

"Marvin, your forehead is bleeding."

"I'll be alright! Who was that fool?"

"That was Bob White, Rozell's husband."

"Did he hurt you or Rozell?"

"No! But, no thanks to you!"

"Shit woman! What did you expect me to do when I was looking down the barrel of a shotgun? Woman, I almost peed on myself!"

"To tell you the truth, Marvin… I did pee on myself," Iris said, chuckling. "And to be honest, from the way you smell, I think you might've pooped on yourself."

"I must've stepped in some dog shit," Marvin responded, embarrassed.

"Well, let's go inside so I can wrap something around your head before you bleed to death."

While Iris was looking for something to tie around his wound, Marvin was surprised to see the large hole in the ceiling. Iris found Rozell's apron hanging on a nail and used it to wrap around his head.

Rozell would usually drive Iris home after work, but she was now stranded. It was nearly five o'clock in the morning and Iris did not want to worry Sarah and Lilly, so she asked Marvin to drive her home. He obliged and drove her directly home, still wearing only one boot.

When they arrived, Marvin told Iris that he was too exhausted to drive all the way back to Roanoke. He asked her if he could come inside and sleep in a chair, for a couple of hours, before journeying on home.

Iris did not want Marvin to fall asleep behind the wheel of his car and have an accident or get killed. But, neither did she want him to come inside. She could not take the chance of Lilly, and especially Sarah, waking up and discovering a strange man asleep in their house. Iris knew that Marvin's jet-black skin would evoke a strong response from Sarah's deep-seated beliefs. Because of the cruelty that she had suffered as a child, at the hands of Mrs. Mabel Green, Sarah believed that all dark-skinned people were evil and that they could bring evil spirits into her home.

Iris told Marvin to park his car in front of the house and to sleep in it, but to try to be gone within an hour. Marvin reluctantly agreed to her terms. Before Iris could EXIT his car, he told her to wait a few moments because he wanted to ask her something.

"Iris, are you married or do you have a boyfriend?"

"I don't have a husband or a boyfriend. I was once engaged, but that was many years ago. He was killed when he was serving in the military. I haven't courted anyone since he died."

"Why? You're such a pretty lady."

"Marvin… after what you've gone through tonight, dealing with Rozell and me, I'm going to tell you the truth. I was pregnant with his child when he died. I stood over his casket and promised him that I would never date another man until our daughter, Samantha, was grown and had left home."

"Is she still living at home?"

"No, she's away at college."

"So, now can you date?"

"I guess so. But, my desire for dating has just vanished."

"Iris, the true reason I travel fifty miles to and from Roanoke every weekend isn't just to teach you and Rozell how to dance. It's because I'm in love with you. My flirting with other women, in the café, was just to make you jealous. Be my girlfriend and let me put that spark back into your life! I'm not just good at dancing!"

Before Iris could tell Marvin that she was not interested, he reached over in an attempt to kiss her. The stench of morning breath exuded from his chapped lips and snaggletooth mouth. In disgust, Iris forcefully pushed him away and opened her door. She briefly hesitated before jumping out and running into the house, leaving him alone in his car.

Later that same morning, Iris looked out of the window to see if

Marvin's car was still parked in the yard. She was planning to take him a cup of freshly brewed coffee to start him safely on his sojourn back to Roanoke, but he was already gone.

Iris would have to find another man to teach her how to dance or to put that spark back into her life because Marvin never returned to Cleo's Place again.

CHAPTER 18

Samantha often wrote home asking Iris to send her more and more money. Although Samantha considered Iris good enough to request money from, she refused to share any information with her mother about her professors, friends, boyfriends, grades, or plans to visit home during the holidays.

In one of her letters, Samantha sent a picture of herself wearing a red dress and black heels. Her hair was silky and hung far below her shoulders. She had gotten much taller and heavier than when she had first left for college.

The three Jackson women silently stared at Samantha's picture until Iris broke their silence and said, "Samantha took her size after her granddaddy, Henry."

A week before Thanksgiving, Iris received another letter from Samantha. In it, she wrote that she was unable to come home for Thanksgiving or Christmas and hoped that everyone would understand. Samantha claimed that she was behind on two term papers and was going to use the holidays to complete them. She, however, promised that she would be home to visit during the spring.

Sarah was extremely disappointed that Samantha was not coming home for the holidays. She had planned to cook all of her favorite foods—homemade cakes, pies, and candies—and play Gin Rummy into the wee hours of the morning. Nevertheless, Iris and Lilly understood that Samantha's grades were more important than her coming home. Besides, they did not think Samantha needed to get any fatter by lying around the house eating with Sarah.

Rozell quit working at the café in order to spend more quality time with her husband, Bob. Lilly eagerly replaced Rozell because Iris would certainly need some help preparing for a Christmas party that was being held at Cleo's Place. Since Samantha was not coming home to visit, Iris and Lilly could devote all of their energy to hosting their upcoming event.

Mr. Bradley Scott, the white boss at Carrolton Georgia Steel Plant, annually sponsored the huge party for his colored employees. Most of the steelworkers were heavy drinkers, had big appetites, and were known to get a bit rowdy when inebriated. This caused most establishments to host them only once before banning them from ever returning. However, the Jackson's felt that the extra money was worth the risk of accepting the job.

Because of the large amounts of food that needed to be cooked, Lilly and Iris asked Sarah to assist them. However, even with Sarah's help, a lot of work would still need to be done.

Three days before the big event, Iris closed the café to customers so that they could cook the large amounts of food. Sarah, Lilly, and Iris were cleaning tubs of chitterlings and collard greens when Rozell suddenly walked into the café to beg for her old job back. She claimed that she had grown claustrophobic of being at home. Lilly and Iris welcomed Rozell back with open arms, but Sarah teased that peg-legged Bob must have begun to bore her to death.

On the night of the party, pots of collard greens cooked with ham hocks, several pounds of chitterlings, containers of neck bones, dishpans of coleslaw, potato salad, and candied sweet potatoes awaited the arriving guests. Jugs of moonshine and punchbowls of spiked eggnog were on a long table in the corner.

Several metal ashtrays and bowls of mixed nuts were on the bar. White tablecloths covered the round tables, which had utensils, plates, tumblers, and plenty of bottles of hot sauce and ketchup. Green garlands and red bows decorated the chairs. Music blasted loudly from the jukebox as everyone began to dance, eat, and drink the night away.

As long as the colored people remained on their side of the river and did not venture near the white people's side of town—except to clean their nice homes, wash their dirty clothes, cook their tasty meals, and nanny for their snotty-nosed children—whites did not care about how much noise they made. According to southern whites, the only time a nigger was a "good" nigger is when he or she was basically working for pennies. In all actuality, the white community of Crosstown wanted the coloreds to go back to Africa, drink themselves to death, or kill each other off. But according to southern blacks, the white community was just racist bigots who would have to keep waiting and wishing because colored people were in this country to stay.

By nine o'clock p.m., most of the steel workers had already arrived at Cleo's Place for the Christmas party. Two of the guests were Iris' former classmates, the twin sisters named Hattie and Mattie. They graduated a year earlier than she had from Mrs. Cora Mae's school. They were now much older and not nearly as pretty as Iris had remembered them. Hattie and Mattie left Crosstown immediately after graduating and moved to Carrollton to work at the steel plant. They both had married and divorced their abusive husbands and each had, also, birthed twin daughters.

But Iris did not have any grandiose events in her life to brag about. Her dream of going to college was stifled when she became a teenage mother. The only man that had ever told her that she was pretty or even tried to kiss her, besides her beloved Sam, was the toothless Marvin Brown.

Iris believed that the promise she made to Sam, after his death, about never loving or being with another man had put a curse on her. It was a promise Iris wished she had never made. If not for the little excitement that she received from working at the café, she would have been a great candidate for a nunnery.

Iris was hoping to avoid speaking to the twins, but she was not so lucky. As Iris turned around with a pan of coleslaw in her hands, one of them was holding a glass of eggnog and obviously inebriated. She was screaming Iris' name over the loud music.

"Hi, Iris."

"Hi, Mattie."

"I'm Hattie," she said, pointing. "Mattie is sitting at that table over there."

"I'm sorry," Iris apologized. "After all these years, I still can't tell you two apart."

"I haven't seen you since we were in school," Hattie slurred. "Are you married?"

"No, but I have a daughter named Samantha," Iris answered.

"We heard you got knocked up," Hattie grinned. "I guess you're no better than the rest of us, huh?"

"Excuse me, Mattie," Iris said purposely calling her the wrong name. "I'm busy right now. I'll have to talk to you later. Those folks over there are waiting for their coleslaw."

Sarah asked Lilly if she would drive her home so she could go to bed. She told her that she was tired from a long day of preparing for the party and that she had consumed too much spiked eggnog, causing her to become intoxicated.

Lilly set the last pan of candied sweet potatoes on the counter before asking Iris, Rozell, and Bob—who had ridden his tractor to the party in order to spy on Rozell—if they would be responsible for the patrons while she drove Sarah home. Despite Bob's constant complaints of him too being ready to call it a night, Iris and Rozell promised they would do their best. Within moments of Lilly and Sarah leaving, Bob also left. Iris and Rozell were the only two who remained at the café to calm the noisy, drunken steelworkers.

Around three o'clock on Sunday morning, Iris unplugged the jukebox and announced that the party was over. Although the steelworkers were disappointed that the party had ended, what they did next took Iris and Rozell completely by surprise. They were unaware that it was a tradition for the steelworkers to end their yearly Christmas parties with a food fight.

Every man and woman in the café began to throw food at each other. They tossed leftovers from their plates and bowls onto the walls and floors. They even dumped eggnog on top of each other's heads. There was nothing Iris or Rozell could do to stop the frenzy. They could only shield themselves and wait until the madness subsided. It seemed like an eternity before the steelworkers were too tired and drunk to continue.

By the time they finished, Cleo's Place was in shambles. Food covered the floor, walls, and ceiling. Tables and chairs were turned over. Plates, bowls, and platters were broken and strewn about. Guests—with their clothes, faces, and hair splattered with debris—began to leave just as happily and friendly as when they had first arrived.

Iris and Rozell waited until the last customer was gone before they let out a loud sigh of relief. They chuckled as they slowly glanced around at what looked like a war-torn café.

"It's a mess in here, isn't it?" Iris asked.

"You can say that again," Rozell added. "Are we going to clean it up now?"

"No way!"

"What's Lilly going to say when she sees this catastrophe?"

"I don't know. So, let's go before she comes back from taking Mama home. Besides, I'm tired and I want to get out of here."

"Me, too! I can't wait to drop you off so I can get home to Bob."

"Then let's lock up and get the hell out of here!"

When Iris arrived home, she found Lilly and Sarah in the kitchen. Sarah, who was holding an empty cup, had fallen asleep with her head down on the table. Lilly was brewing a fresh pot of coffee.

Iris stood over Sarah for a while, before Sarah finally noticed her presence. Sarah then awoke with an immense hangover. She began to apologize for her and Lilly having left Iris and Rozell to handle the unruly partygoers.

"I'm so sorry I got drunk and had to leave so early," Sarah slurred.

"And I want to thank you and Rozell for taking over when Mama and I left," Lilly added.

"Lilly, before you praise us too much… you had better wait until you see the café tomorrow," Iris responded.

"What happened?" Sarah asked.

"I don't know where to begin," Iris answered.

"Tell us what happened!" Lilly demanded.

"There was a food fight after y'all left," Iris answered. "There was nothing Rozell or I could do to stop it! The place is a huge mess!"

"Is it real bad?" Sarah asked.

"Yes… It's very bad," Iris responded.

"We shouldn't have left y'all by yourselves," Sarah said apologetically.

"Just forget about that mess for right now," Lilly said. "We'll get some much needed rest and go over to clean it up later."

Lilly finished brewing the coffee before saying, "Mama, the only reason I've kept the café going this long was because we needed the money. I was hoping that we could save enough to one day build us a dream home, but that seems impossible now. I'm now content with living right here in this house. It's the only home I've known. Heck… some people are homeless. Lilly hesitated before continuing, I've also kept it open so if Cleo ever came home, his café would still be waiting for him. But, it's been years since we've even heard a peep out of him. I've sadly faced the fact that Cleo is probably dead and we more than likely will never see him again."

"If my baby boy is dead, may he rest in peace," Sarah said tearfully. "But as for me, I'll never give up hope of seeing my son again until the day I take my last breath."

"I'm sorry, Mama," Lilly responded. "I shouldn't have said that about my brother. I, too, hope to see him again."

For the first time since they had driven Cleo into the dark backwoods, Sarah reluctantly realized that the chances of her ever seeing Cleo again were slim to none. She now needed to retreat to her bedroom so she could privately nurse her reopened wounds.

Sarah staggered out of her chair and walked toward the kitchen door before turning to Lilly and saying, "I know you loved your brother. He left that café to you because he trusted you to do the right thing. I'm sure if Cleo could send you a message, he would tell you to follow your heart."

* * * * *

Later in the evening on that same day, Sarah was desperately trying to pull her old lumpy mattress off the bedsprings as Lilly and Iris looked on.

"What are you doing?" Lilly asked.

"Don't you see? I'm trying to get this mattress off my bed! Don't just stand there! Help me!" Sarah responded.

"Why?" Iris asked.

"If you do what I say, you'll find out," Sarah said.

Lilly and Iris lifted Sarah's mattress and laid it on the floor. Sarah sat on top of the mattress and began to pull out an extremely dirty pillowcase. It was stuffed inside the crevices of the old mattress. Sarah instructed Lilly and Iris to untie the pillowcase and dump out its contents.

Lilly and Iris' eyes almost popped out of their sockets when they saw the rolls of money falling out of the pillowcase. They began to jump up and down while screaming at the sight of so much money. Sarah, unimpressed by their showmanship, cried out for them to stop.

"Please, please, stop! My head hurts!"

"Sorry, Mama," Lilly said, breathless.

"Lilly, I want you and Iris to take this money and use it to build us the best damn colored folks' home in Crosstown, Georgia."

"Are you sure?" Lilly asked.

"Just as sure as this headache I got," Sarah replied.

"Where in the hell did you get all this money, Mama?" Lilly asked.

"I'm only going to tell y'all once so y'all had better listen carefully."

"Mama, we are all ears," Iris said excitedly.

"Iris," Sarah began, "remember when we found Mr. Parker James dead?"

"Yes, I remember! I don't think I'll ever forget."

"Tell Lilly about the letter Mr. James left for Dr. Baxter. Do you remember us reading it before I gave it to him?"

"Yes, I remember," Iris again uttered.

"I didn't ask you if you remembered. I want you to tell Lilly what the letter said," Sarah demanded.

Iris then recited what she remembered from the letter those many years ago.

"I think that's pretty much all it said, Mama," Iris responded.

"Close enough," Sarah said, laughing. "Girls… you're looking at the person who found his money."

"So it was true," Iris said, surprised. "That old man was rich after all."

"I'm not surprised that Mr. James was rich," Lilly said. "He paid Mama practically nothing for working for him all those years and he never bought anything new, not even clothes. I bet there're some old timers in Crosstown who're still looking for Mr. James' money."

"Well, Hell can freeze over and they'll never find it because I got every penny," Sarah said proudly. "I consider it my payback for him using me for his selfish pleasure for all those years."

"Mama, how did you know where to look?" Iris asked. "Or was he just teasing the other folks and had already given you his money?"

"He should've given it to me, but he didn't," Sarah said passionately. "Out of all those many years that I worked for that man, being a slave to his every wish and even like a wife to him, I wasn't good enough for him to leave me his money. All he left me was this raggedy house and his mule. But, he gave me a clue to where he hid his money when he was angry with me because I didn't bake him a fresh batch of biscuits for breakfast one day. He was so pissed that he slipped up and shouted that he would take his money to his grave before he would ever leave me one red cent!" Sarah continued, "I may not be that educated, but I'm not stupid either. Parker James gave me another clue when he gave Dr. Baxter some money to purchase the coffin that he used to keep in the corner of his bedroom. I knew if he was going to take his money to his grave, it must be hidden in that darn coffin! And damn it… I was right!"

As Sarah began to stuff the wads of cash back into the dirty pillowcase, the vengeful elation she was feeling was evident to both Lilly and Iris. Although they were stunned by her revelation, they admired her strength and reveled in her vindication.

Sarah continued, "One day, I gave Parker James just a little more Paregoric than Dr. Baxter had prescribed. When he was sound asleep, I carefully pulled up the padding from the bottom of his coffin and there his money was!" Sarah briefly paused before asking, "Iris, do you remember me making you go on to school on the day that we found him dead?"

"Yes," Iris recalled. "I still remember that day because Mrs. Cora Mae asked me why I was so late for class and I didn't say a word because I promised you that I would keep his death a secret."

"Well… after you left, I removed his money and brought it home," Sarah added. "Then, I ran back to town to tell Dr. Baxter that Parker James was dead and that he had left a letter for him."

"Unbelievable," Lilly said, flabbergasted.

"Those stupid white hicks destroyed that store and wasted their time looking for the money that I already had!" Sarah gloated with a bittersweet smirk.

CHAPTER 19

When Iris awoke, Lilly and Sarah were already dressed and in the kitchen. Lilly shouted, telling Iris to hurry up and get out of bed because they had some important decisions to make.

Iris forced herself out of the bed and joined Sarah and Lilly in the kitchen.

"Lilly, please tell me I wasn't dreaming when we counted all that money that Mama had hidden in her mattress," Iris pleaded.

"It definitely wasn't a dream," Lilly replied. "I helped you count every dollar. It came up to twenty thousand dollars!"

Sarah, Lilly and Iris held hands and danced around in a circle as they joyfully chanted, "We're rich! We're rich!" They did not stop until they were out of breath. They then sat down at the table.

"Starting this morning, we're going to focus all of our attention and energy into building us a new home," Sarah said.

"What about the mess at Cleo's Place?" Iris asked. "Don't we need to clean it up first?"

"Forget about that mess," Lilly said. "We'll hire someone else to clean it up. Mama's right… let's close the café for a while and focus on building us a new house."

"Where do we start?" Iris inquired.

"With a contractor," Sarah answered.

"Where in the world would we get a contractor from?" Iris asked.

"Rozell's husband, Bob White, knows one that he used to work for. If I'm not mistaken, I think it's called Conrad Davis Building Company,"

Sarah replied. "Bob told me that they're the best in town when it comes to building a house."

"Mama, that white man is known in this town as a crook," Lilly said. "He can't be trusted when it comes to doing business with colored folks. He'll fool them into letting him finance and build their house, but if they miss one payment, he'll take their house along with their land."

"You're preaching to the choir," Sarah said, smiling. "I know he's a crook."

"Then why would we hire him to build us a home and lose everything we've worked so hard for?" Lilly asked.

"We won't lose a damn thing," Sarah said. "Those colored folks that Mr. Conrad cheats out of their land and homes don't earn enough money from their crops to keep up their high payments. They forget about the slow times when their crops don't yield much profit. We have an advantage over those other coloreds because we have enough money to pay for our home in cash." Sarah continued sternly, "For now, our money is a secret that we must keep to ourselves because Mr. Conrad will try to make a fool of us, too! When we go down to see him, we must make him think that we're just some dumb niggers who were fortunate enough to inherit some land! But, let's make him think that the only income we have is from the café. He'll think we are some fools who are trying to live well above our means and that we are easy prey to take advantage of."

Lilly, now comprehending Sarah's plan, said, "Because he'll assume that he'd own our house when we can't make the high payments. Heck, he'll probably think we won't be able to make it to the second payment before being evicted and our stuff thrown out on the ground."

"Lilly, now you're using your head," Sarah responded. "After breakfast, let's ride downtown and see when Mr. Conrad can meet with us."

The Jacksons knew that it was vitally important to keep their money a secret from Mr. Conrad. They could not divulge it until it was necessary.

Sarah believed that the white people of Crosstown—whom she called rednecks and who she was certain still remembered her from the days when she worked for Mr. Parker James—would come in the middle of the night, tie them up, ransack their house, and rob them of their money. She knew it was plausible that they might even murder all three of them. Sarah felt that the white folks, just as they had done with the infamous prostitute, Miss Wilma Lee, would feel like they had gotten exactly what they deserved.

* * * * *

With their plan agreed upon, the three Jackson women went down to Mr. Conrad's office. Since Sarah had mastered the skills of negotiating and bullshitting with white folks, Lilly and Iris decided to let her do all of the talking.

Sarah, Lilly, and Iris were the first people waiting in line to see Mr. Conrad. Although they arrived first, two white couples that arrived after them were invited into his office before them.

Mr. Conrad's son, Conrad Jr., was grinning from ear to ear. He was wearing a pair of khaki pants that were so tight that they were stuck in the crack of his butt. He informed the Jacksons that his father would now see them.

Sarah, Lilly, and Iris followed Conrad, Jr. into his father's office where cigar smoke filled the air. Mr. Conrad was seated at his desk, with his feet propped on top, puffing on a cigar. His son told them to have a seat. Sarah sat in the chair closest to Mr. Conrad's desk.

"Daddy, these are the three women who want us to build them a new house."

"Thanks son! You can now go back to stacking those papers."

"Yes, Daddy."

“Now, ladies,” Mr. Conrad began, “what can I do for you?”

“My name is Sarah Jackson. This here is my daughter, Lilly, and my granddaughter, Iris. We want you to build us a new house.”

“First, you must own some land,” Mr. Conrad explained.

“We do own some land,” Sarah responded.

“You do?” Mr. Conrad asked, surprised.

“Yes, sir,” Sarah answered.

“Where’s your land?” Mr. Conrad inquired.

“It’s all that land that Mr. Henry and Mrs. Emma Boggs once owned,” Sarah replied.

“I remember Henry and Emma Boggs,” Mr. Conrad recollected. “Those Boggs owned a lot of land. Didn’t they have two kids? What ever happened to those nice folks?”

“Their son, Sam, died fighting in the war,” Sarah answered. “And they moved to Detroit several years ago.”

“Sorry to hear that,” Mr. Conrad responded.

“Thank you,” Sarah said. “After their son died, Mr. Henry eventually fell ill and died.”

“Is their daughter dead?” Mr. Conrad asked.

“No, sir,” Sarah answered. “Their daughter, Belinda, still lives in Detroit with Mrs. Emma.”

“Now tell me again, Sarah,” Mr. Conrad grimaced. “How did this land come into your possession?”

"Their daughter, Belinda, gifted it to my granddaughter, Iris, and my great-granddaughter, Samantha."

"Why?" Mr. Conrad asked, nonplused. "That's a lot of land for some colored folks to own."

"It's a long story," Sarah responded. "But, it's true. You can check the courthouse records. It's in Iris and Samantha's name. Look up the name Iris Jackson and you will see that she pays the taxes on the property."

"You can be sure that I'll do just that," Mr. Conrad said.

The three Jackson women now had Mr. Conrad's undivided attention. He took his feet off of his desk, sat up straight in his leather chair, and squished his cigar in an ashtray.

Sitting in his office were three women who owned acres of land that he secretly wanted for himself. Unbeknownst to Mr. Conrad was the fact that Sarah, Lilly, and Iris already knew what he was plotting. They clearly comprehended that he was gambling on them ultimately losing both their house and their land to him. They were well aware that if they missed one payment that he would have them evicted and sell their dream home to some rich white family. Mr. Conrad had cheated so many other colored people out of their hard earned land and money that he was positive that the Jacksons would be no different.

"Son," Mr. Conrad called, "get Sarah a cup of coffee."

"No, thank you," Sarah intervened.

"What about you two gals sitting over there so quiet?" Mr. Conrad asked.

"No, sir," Lilly and Iris responded.

"Now Sarah, tell me some more about that house you want my company to build for y'all," Mr. Conrad said.

"Well," Sarah began, "we want a house with a living room, dining room, kitchen, three bedrooms, a bathroom, and definitely a large front porch."

"Wow… slow down there, Sarah," Mr. Conrad suggested. "Let's not get too ahead of ourselves. It's going to take a lot of money to build that kind of house. I've been in this business a long time and not even some of us white folks have that kind of fancy house. Are you sure you'll be able to make those monthly payments?"

"Our café makes a pretty good living," Sarah responded.

"You talking about that hangout, Cleo's Place?" Mr. Conrad asked.

"Yes, sir," Sarah answered.

"Hell, I didn't know you Jacksons owned your own business," Mr. Conrad said.

"I told you that, Daddy," Conrad Jr. interrupted.

"Quiet boy," Mr. Conrad commanded. "We'll take the job and do a damn good one. My construction company has never been prejudiced against green money. I'll have my architect draw up some blueprints for your approval. You should receive a contract within the next two weeks."

"That will be just fine," Sarah said.

"Ladies, just one more thing before we conclude... I want to clarify that if you're late on or miss more than two payments, I'll have the legal justification to repossess the house and the land it's built on," Mr. Conrad reiterated.

"We fully understand," Sarah said.

"Now that that's clear, Junior please show these lovely ladies to the door," Mr. Conrad said, relighting his cigar.

* * * * *

The Jacksons new house would be built on the same plot of land where the Boggses' house once stood. Their old homestead had been bulldozed and removed.

Sarah, Lilly, and Iris' new house would have a large yard in which they could plant peach trees, flowers, vegetable gardens, and sweet potato patches. The area where three tall oak trees already stood, shading Sam and Mr. Henry's graves, would be expanded into a family cemetery that was large enough to one day encompass the graves of not only the Jackson women, but Mrs. Emma and Belinda. The creek, where Iris and Sam conceived Samantha on their favorite blanket, would be a place where Sarah could fish.

There were rumors spreading, among the white residents of Crosstown, that three colored women were having a huge house built. They were wondering how these three poor women acquired enough money to erect a home of that magnitude. Some speculated that Sarah must have stolen Mr. Parker James' money while he was on his deathbed. Others concluded that the Jackson women were just three more niggers trying to live well beyond their means. Many secretly felt the same way as Mr. Conrad Davis—that it was inevitable and just a matter of time before Sarah, Lilly, and Iris lost their land and house to a wealthy white family.

Crosstown's colored people were not any better than the white people with their envious gossiping. Instead of being happy for them, they were also spreading unfounded rumors. They were saying that Sarah murdered Mr. Parker James, the father of her four children, as he slept, and that she had forged the letter to Dr. Baxter.

Nevertheless—Sarah, Lilly, and Iris were just beginning to accomplish their goals. Would they finally achieve all they had hoped, planned, and worked so hard for? Or were disappointment, dreams deferred, and death lurking in the shadows?

CHAPTER 20

Samantha was coming home for a two-week vacation before returning to college. She informed Iris that her train would be arriving at 8:35 in the morning. However, Iris arrived thirty minutes earlier than Samantha's scheduled time so she could have a clear view of her daughter as soon as she stepped off the train.

Iris was sitting alone on a bench near the station's platform, anxiously waiting. Her hair was styled in a bun that only older librarians would wear. She was dressed in one of her old, but best, housedresses and a pair of fairly new shoes. She was wishing that she had worn a heavier coat and a pair of gloves because it was extremely windy and unusually cold. Even though her hands and feet were beginning to feel numb, Iris decided that sitting where she could see Samantha getting off the train was more important than going inside to the warm waiting room.

This should have been a happy day for Iris, but this train station held so many sad memories. Every time she was at this particular train station, old thoughts of the last time she ever saw Sam alive haunted her. She could never forget the day that she accompanied Mr. Henry, Mrs. Emma, and Belinda to see Sam off to basic training. Neither could she forget Mrs. Emma insisting that she walk behind Sam so that he could use his milky complexion to pass for white.

At 8:15 a.m., the sound of an approaching train could be heard in the far distance. Iris asked a colored man, who walked out on the platform dressed in a porter's uniform, if that was the 8:35 train. The porter confirmed that it indeed was and stated that it was twenty minutes ahead of schedule. As the sound of the train got closer, Iris' heart began to beat faster from the anticipation of seeing her daughter.

The train then came to a screeching halt, covering the platform with clouds of steam. Well-dressed white—and even colored—men, women, and children stepped off the train onto the platform. But, Samantha was nowhere in sight.

The children were teasing each other and playing tag while the adults mingled and talked as they waited for their luggage. Iris felt uncomfortable and out of place around people who did not talk, look, or dress like the regular people she was used to. She regretfully realized that she, too, could have been one of those well-groomed, educated people if she had listened to and followed Sarah's advice. Instead, Iris was now an aging, slightly plump, woman with no man to love or protect her.

Iris was about to leave the train station because she reasoned that Samantha must have either missed her train or decided not to come home. As she prepared to leave—a tall, slender, and sophisticated-looking white girl, dressed in a tailored blue suit and high-heels, suddenly stepped off the train. When Iris realized it was her daughter, she stepped back to get a better look at the beautiful and polished Samantha. They then gave each other a big hug.

"Waiting for someone?" Samantha teased.

"Samantha!" Iris screamed joyfully. "Welcome home!"

"Thank you," Samantha nonchalantly replied.

"You've turned into such a beautiful, young woman. I can't wait until Lilly and Mama see you. They won't believe you're the same person in that picture you sent us. You're so thin! I almost didn't recognize you!"

"I lost a lot of weight."

"I felt your ribs when I hugged you. I better get you home so Mama can put some meat on your bones."

"I don't ever plan to gain that much weight again."

"Well, fat or skinny, we love you and we've missed you!"

Iris gave the colored porter a dollar to put Samantha's heavy luggage into the trunk of the car. Embarrassed by her mother's cheapness, Samantha gave the man some additional money.

On the drive home, Iris talked nonstop about some of the things that had transpired since Samantha had left Crosstown. She told Samantha that they had sold some of the land that they inherited from the Boggses to their friends, Bob and Rozell White, and Sarah's friend, Mr. Tom Willis. Iris eagerly told Samantha how they were going to become their new neighbors. However, the more Iris talked, the less interested Samantha seemed.

"I can't wait until you see how our new home is coming! After supper, I'll drive you, Lilly, and Mama down there so you can see it for yourself. When you come to visit again, we'll be living in our new house. You'll have your own room."

"I'm very tired. I just want to get to the house and rest."

"We can wait until tomorrow if you're too tired to go today."

"That would be much better."

"Tell me about being a college girl?" Iris asked, trying to break the silence. "Do the white and colored students get along?"

"Quite well," Samantha responded. "Many black and white students are best friends. Some even date each other."

"Times have really changed. How about the teachers? Do they treat the white children better than the colored?"

"The students are not children. They are young adults. On campus, we are not called coloreds anymore. We refer to ourselves as black people and the teachers are called professors."

"Sorry! I'll try to remember the differences from now on. I never lived in the world you're in now! You're lucky."

Iris and Samantha continued their journey home in silence until Iris found the courage, even if she were going to be embarrassed by Samantha again, to ask her one more question.

"Samantha, do you have a boyfriend?"

"Yes, I do."

"Tell me about him. What's his name?"

"I'll answer all of your questions about my boyfriend when I tell Mama and Lilly so that I don't have to repeat myself."

When Iris and Samantha arrived home, Sarah and Lilly were busy cooking. They almost knocked each other down trying to be the first to hug Samantha.

"Look at my beautiful granddaughter!" Lilly screamed. "Mama, isn't she pretty?"

"She's as pretty as a sunset," Sarah agreed.

"Are you happy to be home, sweetie?" Lilly asked.

"Yes, ma'am," Samantha responded. "I'm just a little tired."

"Well, you just sit right here at this table and I'll fix you a plate," Sarah said. "Lilly and I cooked all of your favorite foods like fried chicken and coconut cake for dessert."

"Fix her a big plate," Lilly said. "She needs to put some meat on those skinny bones."

"I'm not hungry," Samantha protested. "I just want to lie down and take a nap."

"I'll put you a plate of food away," Sarah said, disappointed. "Maybe you'll feel like eating it later."

*   *   *   *   *

One evening, after Lilly and Iris returned home from working at Cleo's Place, Samantha and Sarah were sitting at the kitchen table playing Gin Rummy. They invited Lilly and Iris to join them. Iris and Lilly knew that either Samantha or Sarah had something important to tell them because they had never asked them to participate in any of their card games before. They immediately sat at the table as Samantha spread out her cards.

"Gin," Samantha said.

"What's wrong?" Iris asked.

"Don't be afraid to tell us," Lilly assured.

Samantha hesitated before asking, "Do you remember when I didn't come home for Thanksgiving or Christmas?"

"Were you pregnant?" Lilly interrupted.

"Well, is Lilly right?" Iris asked.

"Will you two stop interrupting her," Sarah said. "Go ahead and tell them, Samantha."

"Thanks, Mama," Samantha said. "I wasn't behind on my assignments like I told you. As a matter of fact, I was excelling in all of my courses."

"That's great, Samantha," Iris said.

"But, I'm transferring to the University of California to complete my studies," Samantha continued.

“Why?” Sarah asked. “We can’t come all the way to California to see you walk across the stage and receive your degree. We were looking forward to being at your graduation.”

“I’m sorry, but I’ve made up my mind and I’ll understand if you don’t continue to pay for my tuition,” Samantha said, unable to look Sarah, Lilly, or Iris in their eyes. “I’ll just have to go to school part-time while I work and pay for it on my own. I already have a job waiting for me and I’ve been invited to stay with my best friend, Jenny, and her parents. She’s also transferring to the same university.”

“There’s just one more thing I need to tell you,” Samantha said, pausing for a moment to give Sarah, Lilly, and Iris a chance to take in what she was revealing. “Neither Jenny nor her parents know that I’m black.”

“You’ve been passing for white?” Sarah asked, shocked.

“I’m sorry, Mama,” Samantha cried. “I tried to hang with the black coeds, but they seemed so jealous of me. They were always calling me the white girl or some other hateful names.”

“When did you decide to pretend you were white?” Sarah asked.

“When two white girls, Katie and Marsha, approached me on campus. They asked me why I was hanging around the black students. Their question made me realize that they thought I was white and I could continue to pass if I wanted to. From then on, I became a white person and life has been so much easier for me. I have lots of white girlfriends and boyfriends. I get to go into the best places to shop, eat, and party without being stared at. I got my new job in California just because they think I’m white.” She nervously continued, “Please, Mama, try to understand that this has not been an easy decision for me. Sometimes I cry myself to sleep, knowing that I laugh at some of the jokes that those white students tell about us black people. Until things change, I must do what I have to do to survive in this white man’s world! One day, maybe things will change.”

"What about us Samantha?" Lilly asked. "Are you BREAKING THE CHAIN with us?"

"Never," Samantha responded.

"You say that now," Iris interjected. "What about later? How long will you let your lie go on?"

"Samantha, stop this foolishness before you have to deny me, Lilly, and your own mama!" Sarah said angrily.

"I won't ever deny you," Samantha claimed. "I won't… You'll see."

"I'm very disappointed in you, Samantha," Iris said.

"I'm sorry to disappoint you, but passing for white is going to get me farther in this world than claiming my blackness," Samantha insisted. "Even the whites right here in Crosstown, Georgia treat the light-skinned blacks far better than they do the dark-skinned. Don't you want me to succeed?"

"Not this way," Iris answered.

"I have to agree with Iris and Sarah," Lilly added.

"I've made my decision and I'm not changing my mind," Samantha said defiantly. "Remember… I do own half of my grandparents' land. If you all support me through this last year of college, I'll forfeit my half of ownership to all of you. I can go to the courthouse and take my name off of the deed before I leave."

"After all I've done for you, Samantha," Iris said, hurt and disappointed. "I don't feel like I owe you anything! I had to give up going to college and becoming a teacher to be a mother to you. Now… is this the way you are repaying me? The land you inherited from your Aunt Belinda belongs to you. I'll never take any of that away from you. You're my daughter and it's my responsibility to support you until you finish college. So against my wishes, I'll have to respect your decision. I just hope that one day, you'll come to your senses and return to your roots. But…"

"Iris, don't say something you'll regret," Lilly intervened.

"She's right," Sarah added. "Don't make the same mistakes I did with Rose. Give Samantha a chance. Let's stick by her. It's hard being a colored girl in a white man's world. She'll come back to her roots. Won't you, Samantha?"

"I promise you, I'll stop this charade soon," Samantha said in tears. "One day, I'll gladly shout to the world that I'm black and proud! You'll see!"

"I hope so, Samantha," Iris said, hugging her daughter. "Forgive me for the harsh things I said to you. I didn't mean them. I have never regretted having you. If I had to do it all over again, I wouldn't change a thing. Whatever decision you make, I'll always be here for you. I love you and I always will."

"Lilly and I do, too," Sarah said tearfully. "Don't we, Lilly?"

"We certainly do," Lilly responded, choking back her tears.

"I know you do," Samantha said. "I love you all too."

* * * * *

Taking Samantha back to the train station was one of the saddest days in Iris, Lilly, and Sarah's lives. It was especially daunting for Iris because not only had the memories of her last goodbye to Sam resurfaced, but she was disheartened that Samantha had not gotten a chance to see the new house they were building or to visit her father and grandfather's graves.

Samantha stood on the platform, with the three Jackson women who loved her unconditionally, until it was time for her to board the train. Sarah and Lilly were crying as they hugged her. But for some strange reason, Iris could not bring herself to cry.

As Samantha's train prepared to leave the station—the same one from which Iris had once waved Sam off to his death—she wondered would this also be the last time she would ever see her daughter.

Samantha, wiping tears from her eyes, waved goodbye through the train's small window. Iris began calling out to her while running alongside the train as it slowly moved. Samantha continued staring out of the window—at the three women who had raised her—as the train's engine drowned out her mother's calls. The train then picked up speed, leaving Iris, Lilly, and Sarah behind.

Even after the train rounded the bend and was out of her sight, Iris continued her pursuit—running down the platform, as quickly as any aging and graying woman her age possibly could.

CHAPTER 21

Sarah, Lilly, and Iris were devoting all of their attention to building their new home.

As soon as it was finished, they would no longer have to sleep in the same bedroom, listen to rats playing in the loft, use a pee can for a bathroom, wash clothes in a washtub, or hear rain leaking through the crumbling roof and ceiling as it drips into the same pots and pans they use for cooking. Neither would they have to shield themselves from the cold winter wind seeping through the pasteboard walls while trying to keep warm by sitting extremely close to the fireplace.

In their new home—they would have their own bedroom and a bathroom with a commode, bathtub, and hot-running water. Sarah, Lilly, and Iris would now have many options. They could choose if they prefer to eat in the kitchen or the dining room, lounge in the living room, sit in the rocking chair, or swing on the front porch. They would never have to read by oil lamps and candles again because, unlike their current house, their new home would have electricity.

The Jacksons received notice that the final blueprints for their house were ready for approval. Sarah reasoned that she, Lilly, and Iris should take at least two people to serve as witnesses to their agreement. So, Sarah asked Mr. Tom Willis and Mr. Bob White if they would accompany them to Mr. Conrad Davis' office. Although they both agreed, Bob advised Sarah that it would be best to bring at least one white person just to be on the safe side. Sarah carefully thought about Bob's advice before deciding that the best white person to ask was Mr. Jim Boggs.

This, however, would not be an easy request for Sarah to make. Not only did Mr. Jim detest his twin brother, Mr. Henry, for marrying a colored woman, Mrs. Emma, but he also held deep-seated resentment that they, the Jacksons, now owned land that he believed he should have rightfully inherited.

Sarah mustered up the courage and went to visit Mr. Jim Boggs at his grocery store. After all, things were changing in Crosstown, Georgia. Black and white children were going to the same schools, being taught by both white and black teachers, and some were even becoming best friends. These changes were now, albeit very slowly, forcing some racists to also change. Hopefully, Mr. Jim Boggs would be one of those people. Or would he remain the stubborn, racist, bigot he had always been?

When Sarah walked through the front door, Mr. Jim was assisting one of his customers. Most of his customers were now just a few loyal old-timers. Mom-and-pop stores, such as his, had lost most of their business to newer, larger, and more modern supermarket chains.

Sarah was surprised to see the welcoming expression on Mr. Jim's haggard, frail face when he greeted her.

"Sarah Jackson, I haven't seen you in a long time," Mr. Jim said. "Can I get you a coke? You won't have to pay for it."

"No, thank you, Mr. Jim."

"I heard you're having a house built down on my brother, Henry's, old land."

"Yes, sir! Mr. Conrad Davis is building it for us."

"Sarah, please don't let that man cheat you! Conrad is a known crook, especially when it comes to dealing with colored folks!"

"Mr. Jim… that's exactly why I'm here. Will you go with Lilly, Iris, and me on tomorrow and serve as a witness for the deal we are making with Mr. Conrad? We need a white person to vouch for us… just in case he tries something fishy later on."

"Sarah, I'm going to admit something that I've never told anyone before. Henry was my only brother and because he married a colored woman, I stopped talking to him. Now, he's dead and it's too late to make amends. But, I can do this favor for both him and you. Even though I didn't inherit the rest of my family's land, I will make damn sure that a greedy prick like Conrad doesn't get it! My folks worked too hard, busting their backs, for me to let that happen. Before I let that happen, I'll sell this here store and use my life savings to pay for that house myself!" Mr. Jim then turned his back to Sarah as if he had forgotten that she was even there and mumbled, "My God… the way that I treated Henry and his family… I don't blame Belinda for giving them that land!" He, realizing that he was mumbling to himself, then faced Sarah and sternly said, "So you go on down there and sign that contract. If Conrad tries to underhand you, be sure to let me know!"

"Are you saying you won't go with us tomorrow?"

"Trust me, Sarah! I know Conrad's game better than you do! It's best if you keep my involvement a secret for now."

"Thank you, Mr. Jim," Sarah said. "For now, I'll just have to trust you."

"I won't disappoint you or my twin brother, Henry."

"Thanks again, Mr. Jim," Sarah said, walking towards the door to leave. "I must get going now."

As she turned the doorknob and opened the door, Mr. Jim hollered, "Sarah… can I come down there and visit my brother and nephew's graves sometimes?"

"You're welcome to come by anytime, Mr. Jim," Sarah responded without hesitating or breaking her stride.

Despite his reassuring words, Sarah dismissed all probability that Mr. Jim would stand by her and go against a well-known white man like Mr. Conrad Davis. She reasoned that old age might have softened his heart, but certainly not enough to be a witness for a colored woman.

* * * * *

The next day, Conrad Jr. escorted the Jacksons into his father's office. Mr. Bob White and Mr. Tom Willis were with them. Mr. Conrad was standing behind his desk, looking over their blueprints. He was obviously surprised that Bob and Tom had accompanied Sarah, Lilly, and Iris.

"Good morning ladies… Tom, and Bob," Mr. Conrad said. "Y'all have a seat."

"I hope you don't mind, but I invited Tom and Bob to help us make some decisions because they know a lot about construction," Sarah said.

"When it comes to construction, Tom and Bob are your guys," Mr. Conrad responded. "They've done a lot of work for me in the past. Now… if y'all would just stand over here by my desk, I'll explain your blueprints to you."

Each of them stood around Mr. Conrad's desk as he took out some long strolls of documents. He unrolled them and began to point out the different rooms on the blueprints.

"Sarah, this is the layout of y'all new house," Mr. Conrad said. "It has three bedrooms, a living room, a dining room, a kitchen, one bathroom, and a large front porch. I must say that it's a mighty large house, even for the richest of us white folks and certainly for colored folks. A house like this is going to cost you twenty-five thousand dollars and it'll carry a mortgage payment of approximately three hundred and fifty dollars a month. Are y'all going to be able to afford this much money?"

"We sure will," Sarah answered, looking at Lilly and Iris for confirmation.

"Especially with the money we make at the café," Lilly added.

"Are you sure that place makes that much money?" Mr. Davis sarcastically inquired.

"As we stated in our last meeting, we do quite well," Iris said after being nudged by Bob to speak up.

"You colored women are biting off more than you can chew," Mr. Conrad said. "Can't one of you gals talk some sense into Miss Sarah?"

"When Mama makes up her mind, there's nothing anyone can do to change it," Lilly responded.

"Junior," Mr. Conrad called.

"Yes, Daddy," Conrad, Jr. answered.

"Is the contract ready for the Jacksons to sign?" Mr. Conrad asked.

"I got it right here," Conrad, Jr. responded.

"Since Miss Iris and her daughter, Samantha Boggs, are the owners of the land and Miss Sarah and Miss Lilly are the owners of the café, I'll need all four of your signatures before it's official."

"It'll just be me, my daughter, Lilly, and my granddaughter, Iris, who'll be signing," Sarah responded.

"Oh no, Miss Sarah… I'll need Samantha Boggs signature as well," Mr. Conrad asserted.

"My daughter, Samantha, took her name off of the deed during her last visit home," Iris said.

"That's right," Lilly added as Mr. Tom Willis held her hand tightly. "My daughter, Iris, is now the sole owner of the land."

"Well… then… after you three sign this contract, we'll begin clearing the land and building in a week or so," Mr. Conrad responded.

Because Iris was the most educated of the three Jackson women, she carefully read over the contract before declaring, "It looks good to me."

With that confirmation—Sarah, Lilly, and Iris signed their names on the dotted line.

CHAPTER 22

The construction of Sarah, Lilly, and Iris' new home was finally complete. Although everything seemed favorable between them and Mr. Conrad Davis, Sarah still did not completely trust him. Without any tangible evidence, she sensed that he was concocting something sinister. Sarah just did not know exactly what Mr. Conrad was planning, but considering his well-documented, crooked past, she was probably correct in her analysis.

Lilly and Iris were saving the profits that they earned from Cleo's Place and adding it to Sarah's secret money. They would hide their earnings safely inside of their mattress. They agreed that no one would leave the house unless at least one of them remained home to guard their savings. They could not take the chance of Mr. Conrad learning about their money and having some of his nefarious friends break into their house to rob them.

It was no secret that their café was making a lot of profit. Many of their younger colored customers had stopped working on farms and sought jobs in factories so that they could earn higher wages, allowing them to spend more on entertainment.

One night after closing, Lilly and Iris were too exhausted to clean up the café. Instead, they returned to do it the following day. As they neared Cleo's Place, they could see and smell smoke. Iris surmised that a neighbor was probably burning some trash in a barrel. As they got closer, the smell became even more pronounced.

Iris and Lilly were shocked when they realized that the smoke, which they saw and smelled, was coming from their café. They could still see the footprints on the front door where it had been kicked open, nearly taking it off the hinges. They cautiously walked inside while coughing and gasping for air. Someone had set Cleo's Place on fire. Although still smoldering, it miraculously had not burnt down to the ground.

Their café had been extensively vandalized. It was obvious that some type of sledgehammer or other heavy weapon had been used to break the tables, bar stools, and chairs. Some were heaped into a pile and torched with gasoline. Furthermore, the water in the kitchen sink was left on, causing a flood. Food from the shelves and refrigerator was dumped onto the floor. Cooking utensils, pots, pans, glasses, cups, and plates covered the entire area. Cabinet doors were yanked off the hinges. The already barely-working commode was clogged with flour and corn meal. Even the jukebox was smashed into pieces. A carpenter's axe with a broken handle was still lodged into the counter of the bar, splintering it down the middle.

Lilly and Iris sobbed profusely as they glanced around at the destruction. It would take months and far more money than they had saved to repair Cleo's Place. Their only source of income would have to be indefinitely closed for business. Out of sheer fright and confusion, they decided the best thing to do was to quickly return home and notify Sarah.

When they walked into the house, Sarah could tell by their facial expressions that something was terribly wrong.

"Why are y'all back so early?" Sarah asked. "What's wrong?"

"Mama, something terrible has happened to the café," Lilly said. "Somebody broke in and ransacked the place!"

"Is it bad?" Sarah asked, shocked.

"Mama, it's completely destroyed," Iris responded. "It will take months to replace everything! They even tried to burn it down!"

"Even our beloved jukebox was smashed," Lilly added. "Who would've done such a horrible thing?"

"Do you really have to ask that question?" Sarah responded, visibly irritated. "It was probably Conrad Davis and some of his Ku Klux Klansmen! I've been waiting for him to play his evil hand! We need to report this crime to Sheriff Goodson, who is one of Conrad's right-hand buddies. Then… all we have to do is patiently wait. In a few days, that son-of-a-bitch will be contacting us to come down to his office. When he does, we'll have a surprise for him because we got something that he's not counting on—cash money! Trust me girls! He hasn't beaten us yet!"

"Are you sure, Mama?" Lilly asked.

"As sure as the day is long," Sarah answered.

As Sarah predicted, Mr. Conrad Davis requested that she, Lilly, and Iris meet him at the courthouse in Judge Becky Teal's chambers. Although she had little faith that he would come, Sarah sent Mr. Jack Jones to tell Mr. Jim that she desperately needed him to come to the courthouse by two o'clock.

Sarah, Lilly, and Iris arrived an hour earlier than their scheduled appointment. They brought Mr. Bob White and Mr. Tom Willis with them to serve as witnesses. Sarah was mentally prepared and had envisioned how the meeting would unfold.

Surprisingly, Mr. Conrad was waiting at the courthouse when they arrived. He and three other white men were standing in the hallway talking and laughing with Judge Teal. When the judge saw Lilly, she hurried to greet and hug her.

"Miss Lilly, do you remember me?" Judge Teal asked.

"I don't think so," Lilly responded.

"You were a housekeeper for my parents, John and Christine Cruse. I was just a little girl when you used to babysit my two brothers and me. My last name was Cruse before I married into the Teal family."

"Little Becky Sue Cruse?" Lilly asked, surprised.

"Yes, ma'am… that's me."

"My, how time flies," Lilly said, nonplused. "You've grown up and are now a judge. I'm so proud of you."

"Thank you, Miss Lilly," Judge Teal said, smiling.

"How's your mama and daddy doing?"

"My mother died about six years ago, but Daddy is still trucking along just fine."

"Sorry to hear about your mama passing. Mrs. Cruse was always so nice to me. I'm sure she's in Heaven watching over you."

"Thank you, Miss Lilly," Judge Teal said, redirecting the conversation towards business. "Now, tell me, what brings you down to the courthouse?"

"They're here to see me concerning their new house my construction company just finished building for them," Mr. Conrad interrupted as he handed Judge Teal some papers. "I don't know if you are aware of it, but their café they call Cleo's Place was seriously damaged. It will be out of commission for a very long time."

"No, I wasn't aware of that," Judge Teal responded. "Who told you?"

"Sheriff Goodson," Mr. Conrad answered. "I drove over to the café to see it for myself. It looks bad… real bad. I hope they catch the bastards who did it!"

"I do too," Judge Teal said. "But, what's that got to do with their new house?"

"Well Judge, the café was their only source of income," Mr. Conrad responded. "I highly doubt they'll be able to make their monthly mortgage payments on time. I'm here today to help them by taking their new house off of their hands. I'm willing to offer them a few hundred dollars to keep them afloat."

"Well… I do declare," Judge Teal said.

"I'm not the bad guy here Judge, but I put a lot of work into building that house and they're legally obligated to pay me for it. I must look out for my family and myself. I also have to pay my employees, who have children to feed."

"I understand," Judge Teal said, briefly glancing at the three white men who accompanied Mr. Conrad.

"If I take ownership of the Jackson's new house, I'll sell it to a family that can afford the mortgage payments. That way, I can pay my employees what they're owed. With all due respect, Miss Sarah should thank God that she still owns her old house that Mr. Parker James gave her so she and her family won't be completely out on the street."

"Mr. Conrad, are the papers you handed me related to the Jackson's house?" Judge Teal asked.

"They're the original contract that Sarah, Lilly, and Iris signed," Mr. Conrad responded.

"Let's go into my office so I can read over these papers and see if there's anything I can do to resolve this problem," Judge Teal said.

Everyone followed Judge Teal into her office. She brushed up against her cluttered desk as sat down in a plush leather chair. Mr. Conrad and his three witnesses sat in one corner of the room while Sarah, Lilly, Iris, and their two witnesses sat in the other. They all waited in silence, not once looking at each other. It was as if they were preparing for a boxing match and the judge was in charge of sounding the bell for each corner to come in the middle of the ring to fight. The judge carefully read over the contract twice before finally speaking.

"Lilly, are you the spokesperson for your family?" Judge Teal inquired.

"No, ma'am," Lilly answered, pointing to Sarah. "My mama, Sarah Jackson, will be. I hope you don't mind, but we brought Mr. Tom Willis and Mr. Bob White along as witnesses."

"Not at all," Judge Teal responded. "It's a pleasure to meet you, Miss Sarah."

"Likewise," Sarah responded.

"And who's this lady?" Judge Teal inquired.

"That's my daughter, Iris," Lilly responded. "She owns the land the house was built on."

"Nice to meet you also, Miss Iris," Judge Teal said.

"Thank you, Judge," Iris said.

"Mr. Conrad... I assume you'll be speaking for yourself," Judge Teal said.

"That's correct, Judge," Mr. Conrad answered. "These three men, sitting right here, work for me and witnessed the hard work my construction company put into building that house."

"Well, since all of the formalities are over, let's get down to business," Judge Teal said. "Miss Sarah, is it true that your café is closed for repairs?"

"Yes, Judge… it is," Sarah answered. "It'll be closed down for at least six months to a year… if not longer."

"Correct me if I'm wrong," Judge Teal began, "but according to this contract, the only thing that would keep you from defaulting on your loan is your café, which is now out of commission. As disappointing as it might seem, Miss Sarah, maybe you should take the little money Mr. Conrad is offering you."

"Is that our only option?" Sarah asked.

"It is," Judge Teal responded. "That's unless you're able to pay the twenty-five thousand dollars, in full, today. That's a lot of money. Are you prepared to do that?"

"Yes, ma'am… I am," Sarah responded.

Sarah took several rolls of wrinkled hundred-dollar bills out of the large black purse that she was tightly clutching. She placed the bundles of money, tied together with strands of cloth torn from old rags, on top of Judge Teal's mahogany desk. Mr. Conrad and Judge Teal were flabbergasted by Sarah's quick response.

"Well, Miss Sarah… I don't think any of us were expecting that," Judge Teal said, smiling. "Mr. Conrad, come up here and count your money so we can verify that it's all there."

"S-s-sure," Mr. Conrad stuttered, still in denial at what he was seeing.

"It's all there," Sarah said, watching him carefully.

As Mr. Conrad began to count the money, Mr. Jim walked into Judge Teal's chambers and sat in the Jacksons' corner.

"Jim Boggs… what are you doing here?" Mr. Conrad asked.

"Sarah invited me," Mr. Jim answered. "I'm here just in case she needs me to loan her some money."

Mr. Conrad and his three witnesses looked back and forth at each other. The men mumbled something indecipherable to one another as Mr. Conrad grunted under his breath.

"She's doing quite well by herself," Judge Teal responded with a chuckle. "Seems as though Miss Sarah was ready for whatever came her way today. I've never seen a person prepared to pay this much money at one time. What bank did you rob, Miss Sarah?"

"My daughter, Lilly, and my granddaughter, Iris, saved every penny they made at Cleo's Place," Sarah said with pride. "And Lilly also saved her money she made working as a maid for people like your mama and daddy."

"Well, I'm glad my parents could help," Judge Teal said.

Mr. Conrad continued to count his money until he was satisfied that it was all there. He even returned a hundred-dollar bill to Sarah.

"Mr. Conrad, is all of your money accounted for?" Judge Teal asked.

"Yes, Judge," Mr. Conrad answered, clearly disappointed.

"Then there's no reason why we can't complete the transfer of ownership before my next appointment," Judge Teal responded. "Miss Sarah… if you, Lilly, Iris, Mr. Conrad, and both of your witnesses sign a few papers, we can complete the transfer today."

"That'll be just fine," Sarah responded, looking at Lilly and Iris for reassurance.

"Mr. Conrad… who, among your witnesses, will sign for you?" Judge Teal asked.

"Matthew Taylor, Ed Nelson, and Larry Allen," Mr. Conrad said, pointing to the three white men who accompanied him.

"And for you all, Miss Sarah?" Judge Teal asked.

"I brought my friends, Mr. Bob White and Mr. Tom Willis, with me," Sarah said tearfully. "But, I would also like for Mr. Jim Boggs to be our witness."

"There he is," Judge Teal whispered. "Ask him."

"Mr. Jim, will you be a witness for us?" Sarah asked.

"Miss Sarah, it would be my honor," Mr. Jim answered.

"Now that that's settled, all I need are your signatures on these documents," Judge Teal said. "Miss Sarah, you can take them across the hall to the Probate Office to be filed."

They then stood before Judge Teal as Mr. Conrad signed over the deed to Sarah, Lilly, and Iris' new house. After both sets of witnesses signed their names, Sarah began to cry. Although equally emotional, Lilly and Iris were trying to hold their tears inside.

Mr. Jim motioned as if he were going to comfort Sarah, but then hesitated.

"Thank you, Judge Teal," Sarah said through tears.

"You're most welcome," Judge Teal responded. "As for this case, my work is done. So, if you ladies and gentleman don't mind, I need to get ready for my next appointment."

"Yes… thanks Judge Teal," Mr. Conrad added, visibly perturbed by the Jackson women being the first colored family to beat him at his own game of trickery.

"Lilly, it's good seeing you again," Judge Teal said. "It's been way too long."

"Yes, ma'am… it has," Lilly responded. "Tell your daddy that I said hello."

After lagging behind to talk to Judge Teal, Lilly hurried across the hall where Sarah and Iris were finalizing their paperwork. Although Mr. Conrad and his witnesses were now gone—Mr. Jim, Bob White, and Tom Willis were still there to ensure everything went smoothly. All they needed was Lilly's signature. After she signed her name—three generations of Jackson women walked out of the courthouse the proud owners of a brand-new, fully paid for, home.

As they stood outside, on the steps of the courthouse, Sarah felt compelled to show Mr. Jim her gratitude for him keeping his promise. She wanted to hug him, but feared that he was not yet ready to be that intimate. However, when Sarah went to shake his hand, Mr. Jim instead pulled her close and tightly hugged her. Lilly and Iris briefly observed their interaction before waiting for Sarah in the car.

"Thank you, Mr. Jim," Sarah said. "You don't know how much your support meant to me."

"There's no need to thank me, Sarah," Mr. Jim responded. "I'm the one that should be thankful that you've forgiven me for the way I've treated you in the past and for all those ugly things I said about you colored folks."

"That's now all in the past," Sarah assured him.

"Excuse me, Sarah," Mr. Jim said as he began to walk away. "I hate to rush, but I got to get home because I'm not feeling too well."

"Okay, Mr. Jim," Sarah responded.

As Mr. Jim prepared to get into his car, he looked back at Sarah who was still standing on the courthouse steps. He then smiled before saying, "It's amazing how old age can change a person's heart… isn't it Sarah?"

"Yes… it sure is," Sarah responded. She then paused before saying, "Mr. Jim... please take care of yourself."

Mr. Jim slightly nodded in recognition of her words before slowly driving away.

Sarah, Lilly, and Iris were unaware that when they waved Mr. Jim goodbye that it would be the last time they would see him alive. He died shortly thereafter.

They were also oblivious to the fact that Mr. Jim had mustered up the last of his strength, climbing out of his deathbed, to come down to the courthouse in order to ensure that they did not lose the land that once belonged to his parents and the twin brother, sister-in-law, nephew, and niece that he had shunned for so many years.

CHAPTER 23

During the final days of living in their old house—Sarah, Lilly, and Iris were left with the dreaded task of deciding what personal belongings they wanted to take to their new home and which ones they would leave behind. Their old house, which was gifted to them by Mr. James Parker, would soon be demolished and hauled away.

They decided to leave behind their rusted iron bed frames and the bedsprings in which sharp edges poked into their bodies as they tried to sleep. Neither would they be taking their bedbug-infested mattresses, the dresser with its missing drawer and cracked mirror, the kitchen table and its nonmatching four chairs, nor the cookware that they also used to catch rainwater that leaked from the ceilings. Instead, they decided to replace their old items with new ones.

Iris looked out into the backyard where they had performed many of their housekeeping duties. She saw the black wash pot that once proudly boiled their dirty bed sheets. She glanced at the two aluminum washtubs, one for washing their colored clothes and the other for rinsing them, and the wooden washboard that Sarah would use to scrub the stubborn stains from their garments. Iris also saw where Sarah had planted a vegetable garden many years ago. The old chicken coop was still standing, but its last chicken had long since been eaten. The backyard also held tall peach trees, whose blossoms filled the air with sweet smelling perfume; Iris could almost taste one of Sarah's peach pies that she would bake using the wormy peaches that she picked from the branches.

As Iris continued to look out of the back door, a ripe berry dropped from the huge chinaberry tree. This was the same tree that she would often hide behind when she was afraid or when there was a family argument. Iris reminisced about how she and her aunt, Rose, would sit under that tree and talk for hours during the hot summer evenings. Iris was taken aback when she realized how long ago it had been.

"My sweet aunt, Rose," Iris softly prayed. "Please come home."

Over the years, Sarah rarely mentioned Rose's name. Out of respect, Lilly and Iris refrained from speaking of Rose in Sarah's presence. They were certain that she would have liked to discuss Rose, but her pride and stubbornness would not allow it.

Iris wondered, "Will I end up just like my grandmother, who doesn't know what happened to her own children, Rose and Cleo? Is it possible that I won't know where my own daughter, Samantha, is someday?" She then promised herself, "In my next letter, I'll let Samantha know that I love her and that she's always welcome home."

Although Iris was in deep thought, she could still hear Sarah and Lilly's conversation.

"Most of my clothes are too old and raggedy," Sarah said. "I'm going to buy me some new ones."

"You and me both," Lilly agreed.

"I can't find my lace handkerchief that John gave for my birthday," Sarah complained, searching for it. "It seems as though it just disappeared."

"Sorry, Mama," Lilly responded. "I know how much that handkerchief meant to you."

"It's okay," Sarah reasoned. "I can't take it with me to the grave."

"Besides our family album and the Bible, there's not much here that I want to take," Lilly said. "What about you?"

"Just my old rocking chair," Sarah responded.

As Iris went to join Sarah and Lilly in the kitchen, she suddenly stopped at the door of their spare bedroom. At the insistence of Mr. Parker James, this was where many of Sarah's colored boarders once slept. Long had passed since the days when it had been converted into a parlor so Sarah could entertain guests. It was now a storage room full of rusted furniture, garbage bags of trash, and moldy clothes.

Beads of sweat formed on Iris' forehead as she slowly opened the door and walked inside. Cobwebs were hanging from every corner of the ceiling. The pee-stained mattress—where her father, George Dawson, used to have sex with her grandmother, Sarah, and her mother, Lilly—leaned against the crumbling wallpaper. It was the same mattress where Mr. Charlie Sweet and her aunt, Rose, made love before leaving town, never to be heard from again. But, this soiled mattress held another dirty secret. It was there that Mr. Joe Fish raped Iris, taking her innocence. The memories of what he had done to her, coupled with the stench of his fishy body odor, bombarded her already clouded mind.

Iris stared at the moldy clothes, which had now turned to rags, scattered across the dusty floor. It was at that moment that she finally realized that it was just a bedroom. There was no reason for her to be scared because it had no power to harm her, Sarah, or Lilly ever again. Iris felt solace in her forgiveness of the bedroom where so much wrong, hurt, and disappointment had transpired. She reckoned that the fault belonged to the people who once occupied it and they—George Dawson and Mr. Joe Fish—were long gone. Iris walked out of the bedroom and closed the door, leaving her fears and the old memories behind.

When Iris finally went into the kitchen, Sarah was going through some old papers while Lilly was struggling to pull something out of a hole in the wall.

As Lilly reached behind the potbelly stove, she mumbled, "Something is stuck down here." She then giggled, "Maybe it's another bag of Mr. Parker James' money." After several attempts, Lilly finally gave up and declared, "It's probably just one of those many rags that we stuffed in holes to help keep the house warm and those pesky rats out."

Iris sighed with relief when Lilly eventually ceased trying to retrieve whatever was in the hole. That was because Iris knew exactly what was hidden there—her doll, Miss Ann. That hole, in the wall, had served as Miss Ann's makeshift dollhouse for all those many years.

As soon as Lilly and Sarah left the kitchen, Iris finished the task that Lilly had unsuccessfully started. She reached into the crevices of the hole until she felt one of Miss Ann's legs. When she finally pulled Miss Ann completely out, she could see the child-sized blue dress and panties that she was wearing when Mr. Fish molested her peeping through the hole. In Iris' mind, she had pulled her doll to safety. In a weird way, Iris felt by rescuing Miss Ann that she had freed herself from the emotional bondage of her past.

Iris then held Miss Ann close to her chest. She felt the same admiration and love for her old doll as when she was a little girl. As Iris continued to hug Miss Ann, she was momentarily a kid again. But as she turned around, the reflection of her graying hair and wrinkling face quickly bought her back to reality.

Iris continued to stare into the cracked mirror that hung crookedly on the kitchen wall. She was certainly not a child, but an older woman. Nevertheless, she was still elated to have her doll back after so many years of separation. Miss Ann gave Iris renewed hope that she would also see her aunt Rose, uncle Cleo, and even her daughter, Samantha, again.

The three generations of Jackson women were now ready to leave their old house with their most treasured and prized possessions. Sarah had a photo of her oldest son, John, wearing his army uniform, and her old rocking chair. Lilly had the family album and Bible. And Iris had her beloved doll, Miss Ann.

Sarah, Lilly, and Iris had proven to themselves and the naysayers of Crosstown that, together, they could and would weather any storm. They might not have been the most educated of women, but they had the wherewithal to keep from BREAKING THE CHAIN that bound them.

As they began their journey to their new home, Sarah had a sudden thought. She turned and momentarily glanced toward the direction of their old house and mumbled, “I wonder if Cleo and Rose will know how to find us?” However, she quickly reasoned, “Oh, that’s okay. I’m sure someone will tell them.” Sarah then turned her head forward and whispered, “That is... if they’re still alive.”

CHAPTER 24

Two years had passed since the Jacksons settled into their new home. Within that time, Sarah's newly planted peach trees had begun to grow. In another year or two, they would bloom and bear fruit. Her rose garden was also thriving and the vegetable patch was producing more vegetables than they could eat or preserve in jars.

Having purchased some of the Jackson's land, Bob and Rozell had finally finished building and moving into their new house. They now lived next door to the Jackson's. Mr. Tom Willis, having bought half an acre from them, resided in a small bungalow on the opposite side.

The three sets of colored neighbors named their close-knit community Freedom Lane. It was a place where flower gardens and green lawns replaced neatly swept dirt yards and their newly built houses stood among tall oak trees.

They were not only neighbors, but also friends that sincerely cared about each other. They would even nurse one another back to health if one of them were ill and if needed, run errands such as paying bills or buying groceries. They often shared their baked goods, dined together, or just sat on their porches and chatted. On late summer evenings, they would listen to the sounds of crickets and bullfrogs singing by the creek or watch fireflies dancing around in the moonlit sky.

Although seemingly content, they all had skeletons in their closets. Mr. Tom Willis' wife died from tuberculosis before she had the opportunity to move into their new home; Rozell discovered that after years of believing that she was infertile that it was in fact Bob who was sterile; Sarah was reliving the death of her oldest son, John, and wondering if her son, Cleo, and daughter, Rose, were still alive; and Lilly was questioning why Sarah never loved her as much as she did her other children—especially Rose.

Iris was contemplating what life would have been like if Sam had not died. She was speculating, "Would I have finished college and become a teacher? Would Sam and I have gotten married and raised Samantha together? Why doesn't Samantha come home to visit me? Is our relationship strained because she was raised without a father?"

Unlike Sarah and Lilly, Iris did not want to wonder for the rest of her life. She needed answers to her questions before so much time had passed that a wedge was forever formed between her and Samantha or one of their deaths prevented them from ironing out their differences.

* * * * *

Cleo's Place had just recently reopened. Iris decided to take off from work in order to travel to California. She was planning to confront Samantha and hopefully get some answers to the burning questions in her mind. However, because the café was just starting to make money again and she and Lilly were short of help, Iris decided to postpone her travels for another week or so.

However, the day before she was scheduled to leave for California, Iris saw a letter that Sarah had left on the kitchen table. She picked it up and discovered that it was from Samantha. Then she sat down at the table and silently read it.

Dearest family,

I hope this letter finds you well. I'm doing great. I know I've neglected you by not writing more—especially after everything you all have done for me. I'll always love you for that and don't think for one moment that I'm not grateful.

That's why you deserve the truth about the secret I've been keeping and why I've avoided coming home. The two photos in this letter are of my three children. One is of my twin girls, Sarah and Iris. The other photo is of my baby girl, Lilly. I named them after the grandmother, great-grandmother, and great-great grandmother they've yet to meet.

Jeffery and I have been married for several years. We were already married during my last visit home. I lied to you when I said I was moving to California to live with Jenny and her parents. I was actually moving there to start a new life with my husband.

Mama, you must forgive me. Jeffery is white and he and his entire family are under the impression that I'm also white. I've gotten into this web and don't know how to get out of it. Sir Walter Scott said it best when he wrote, "Oh what a tangled web we weave, when first we practice to deceive."

If I told Jeffery the truth, he would divorce me and take my children away. I would never see them again. His family is very rich and powerful.

Please give me time to figure this mess out. I beg of you not to send me any more pictures of you all. Jeffery found some of them and asked me who you were. I had to tell him that you all were my dead father's former maids.

I ask you again, Mama, PLEASE give me the chance to think through this situation.

Love Always,

Samantha

Iris stared at the photos of her granddaughters before rereading Samantha's letter several more times. She replayed each word and syllable in her mind, trying to determine how it all got to this point.

She then heard Sarah come into the house from fishing at the creek. Lilly greeted Sarah in the hallway and together they joined Iris in the kitchen.

"I see you found the letter from Samantha," Sarah said.

"Well… what did it say?" Lilly asked.

“You and Lilly had better read it for yourself,” Iris said. “Here are some pictures she sent.”

Iris handed the pictures to Sarah and the letter to Lilly. When Lilly finished reading the letter aloud, she and Sarah were speechless. They remained silent until Sarah finally spoke.

“Iris, don’t give up on Samantha,” Sarah said. “Continue to let her know that you love her. One day, she’ll return to her roots and bring those beautiful children with her.”

“Thanks, Mama,” Iris said while unsuccessfully trying to mask her disappointment. “You’ve always been the glue that binds us.”

“Don’t let you and Samantha end up like me and Rose,” Sarah pleaded. “I didn’t think I’d ever admit it, but I wish I had a second chance to do a lot of things over. There’s not a day that goes by that I don’t think about my beautiful Rose.”

“She’s right, Iris,” Lilly added, secretly revisiting the notion that Sarah always loved Rose more than her.

Sarah, usually upbeat and active, seemed drained of all of her energy. She stood up from the table and said, “Well with that confession, I’m going to bed.”

“But, it’s still early Mama,” Lilly replied. “Don’t you want to eat supper before you go to bed? I’m getting ready to set the table.”

“I’m not hungry,” Sarah said as she walked out of the kitchen.

CHAPTER 25

Sarah would always wake up before Lilly and Iris. By the time they got out of bed, she would usually be standing over the stove, cooking breakfast. But something seemed different on this particular morning.

When Lilly awoke, the house was very quiet. She assumed that Sarah and Iris were still asleep. Lilly decided to surprise them by cooking a southern-style breakfast.

As Lilly filled their plates with freshly baked biscuits, cheese grits, scrambled eggs, and bacon—she yelled for Iris to tell Sarah that breakfast was ready.

When Iris walked into Sarah's bedroom, she found her covered with only her white cotton sheets. Her quilted bedspread had been completely removed. It appeared as though she might have gotten too warm and had tossed it onto the floor. Sarah seemed extraordinarily still without the slightest movement. The way Sarah was positioned reminded Iris of how Mr. Parker James looked when they found him dead in his bed. Growing more concerned, Iris decided to take a closer look.

"Lilly, come quick!" Iris suddenly screamed. "I think Mama's dead!"

Lilly immediately ran into the room. She found Iris crying and kneeling beside Sarah's bed. Lilly also believed that her mother was dead until she saw Sarah trying desperately to speak.

"She's not dead," Lilly said as she gently rubbed Sarah's cheeks. "Don't talk, Mama. Save your energy. You'll be all right." Lilly then screamed, "Iris, go and get Dr. Baxter!"

"Mama, you just hold on," Iris cried. "I'll be right back with Dr. Baxter!"

"He's not at his office this early," Lilly cried out. "You'll have to drive to his house."

"Okay," Iris replied as she quickly changed out of her nightgown into a housedress that was hanging in Sarah's closet.

"Tell him that Sarah Jackson is very ill," Lilly said. "Now, hurry!"

Crying hysterically, Iris ran from Sarah's bedside and hurried out of the door. She jumped in their old Ford and sped off, flooring it as she left the driveway. Smoke emitted from the engine and tires as she forced the old car to go as fast as it could.

When she finally found Dr. Baxter's house, Iris parked behind his black Cadillac. She frenziedly rang the doorbell. Dr. Baxter was startled when he opened his front door and saw her standing there.

"How can I help you?"

"Dr. Baxter, will you please come to my house? My grandmother, Sarah Jackson, is very ill."

"Is she the woman who used to work for Parker James all those years?"

"Yes, sir. She's my grandmother."

"I have an hour before I'm scheduled to see my first patient. Give me a few minutes and I'll get my medical bag."

"Please, Dr. Baxter! We don't have much time!"

Dr. Baxter then followed Iris back to Sarah's house, driving as quickly as they could. Iris ran in the house with Dr. Baxter trailing closely behind. Iris could see the amazement on Dr. Baxter's face when he saw how well they were living.

Iris led Dr. Baxter directly to Sarah's bedroom. Lilly, still next to her bed, stood up from her chair so that Dr. Baxter could sit down. He took his stethoscope out of his black medical bag and listened to Sarah's heartbeat for what seemed like an eternity. He then motioned for Lilly and Iris to follow him into the hallway.

"Her heart is very weak," Dr. Baxter said. "Miss Sarah is dying."

"Please save my mama!" Lilly said tearfully.

"I wish I could, but there's nothing more I can do," Dr. Baxter responded to a weeping Lilly and Iris. "But miracles do happen! If she makes it through the night, she might get better."

* * * * *

Although Iris tried her best to stay awake all night, she eventually fell asleep around midnight. She was then abruptly awoken by Lilly informing her that Sarah was trying to mumble something. As Lilly and Iris carefully listened, they could hear Sarah calling out for Rose.

With tears flowing down her cheeks, Lilly tightly held Sarah's hand.

"I'm here, Mama," Lilly said, pretending to be her sister, Rose. "Your beautiful Rose is right here by your side."

"Rose, please forgive me," Sarah said, delusional.

"Mama, I forgive you," Lilly replied.

"Rose..." Sarah said before pausing, unable to finish her sentence.

"Yes, Mama," Lilly responded as Sarah took her last breath.

This was one sleep from which Sarah would never awaken. She would never again be the first in the kitchen to cook breakfast. Neither would she be there to fill the air with the aroma of her peach pies baking in the oven. Nor would Lilly and Iris ever hear the sound of her dragging fishing poles as she returned from fishing at the creek.

The Jackson women, who had for so long been three, were now two. Their beloved mother, grandmother, and friend—who had always protected, guided, and supported them—was now dead.

Sarah had gone as far with them as she could; Lilly and Iris would have to go the rest of the way without her.

CHAPTER 26

Sarah had often told Lilly and Iris that upon her death, she wanted to be buried wearing a pink dress and white gloves.

Sarah was not a very religious woman so she had always requested a graveside ceremony in lieu of a church funeral. She wanted to be buried in their family cemetery, where Sam and Mr. Henry Boggs were also laid to rest. Sarah had often spoken of her desire to have Reverend Wade Crowder read Psalm 23 and Miss Carrie Williams sing Amazing Grace.

Although some of Sarah's requests would be easier to fulfill than others, Lilly and Iris were determined to ensure that her last wishes were honored. It would be a simple task to purchase Sarah's burial clothes from a department store in LaGrange or to get Miss Carrie Williams to sing. But, it would not be easy to get Reverend Wade Crowder to deliver the sermon.

Reverend Crowder's wife, Mrs. Louise, was the older sister of Miss Carrie Williams and she did not want her husband in the company of what she termed, "my low-down sister." Mrs. Louise never forgave her sister after she caught her in bed with Reverend Crowder. But, Miss Carrie felt it was Mrs. Louise who had backstabbed her and not the other way around.

It all started when the two sisters were teenagers. The beautiful Miss Carrie was the first to date Reverend Crowder. He always loved and wanted to wed her. However, Miss Carrie was more focused on her future than getting married. When she got an opportunity to leave the farm and attend college, she quickly left Crosstown. Miss Carrie eventually became a teacher and never thought twice about Reverend Crowder again. Mrs. Louise, who was always considered the unattractive sister, was not fortunate enough to go to college. Instead, she stayed behind to care for their aging parents.

In an attempt to mend his broken heart and forget about Miss Carrie, Reverend Crowder began to date her older sister. It was common knowledge that the only reason he married Mrs. Louise was because she got pregnant with his child.

Within a month after their marriage, Mrs. Louise and Miss Carrie's father died. Miss Carrie returned to Crosstown to attend the funeral, but decided to remain home in order to help Mrs. Louise care for their ill mother.

Mrs. Louise was always intimidated at the possibility that Reverend Crowder had never stopped loving her sister. Her fears were soon confirmed when Reverend Crowder and Miss Carrie saw each other again. Although Miss Carrie had abandoned him and Reverend Crowder was now a married man, their old flames burned brighter than ever. They would eventually start an adulterous affair behind Mrs. Louise's back.

Mrs. Louise would often stay overnight at her parent's house, praying next to her ailing mother's bedside. She was even holding her mother's hand when she took her last breath.

According to rumors, Mrs. Louise ran to her house to seek comfort in the arms of her husband. Instead, she walked into their house to find Reverend Crowder and Miss Carrie having sex.

The sight of her husband being intimate with her sister, coupled with the death of both of her parents, was so traumatic that Mrs. Louise miscarried.

After her miscarriage, Mrs. Louise lost all the love she ever had for Reverend Crowder. Nevertheless, she remained his wife in order to punish him. From that point forward, Mrs. Louise refused to cook, clean, or have intercourse with him as retribution for his infidelity. She also started to dress in all black clothes to mourn her dead child. She hated Reverend Crowder so much that, for years, she even refused to speak to him although they lived under the same roof.

Similarly, Reverend Crowder could not bring himself to divorce Mrs. Louise. He blamed himself for her losing their unborn baby.

Sarah had once tried to convince her good friend, Reverend Crowder, to leave his loveless marriage and marry Miss Carrie, the woman he truly loved. When Mrs. Louise found out, she began to hate Sarah just as vehemently as she despised her husband and sister.

Despite Lilly's knowledge of all that had transpired in the past, she was still intent on guaranteeing that Sarah's last wishes were upheld. She and Iris then got in their old car, preparing to do just that.

When she was a small child, Lilly once visited the Crowder's home with Sarah. But it had been so long ago, she could not remember which of the narrow dirt roads they lived on. Finally, in the near distance, Lilly recognized the Crowder's old shotgun house. She then quickly turned in and parked in their yard.

Mrs. Louise was walking from her okra patch, carrying a butcher's knife and a pan of okra. She was wearing a straw hat that had a wide brim. Lilly was surprised that, even after all of these years, Mrs. Louise was still dressing in black clothing.

Lilly and Iris quickly got out of the car. They loudly greeted Mrs. Louise, who glanced toward their direction without responding. She just continued walking to her house, almost tripping over her long dress as she climbed the steps of her porch. Mrs. Louise then opened the torn screen door and went inside.

A few moments later, Reverend Crowder exited his house and stood on the porch. He adjusted his bifocal glasses in an attempt to see who was standing in his yard. Reverend Crowder did not want any uninvited guests to witness his dilapidated home, dying gardens, parched fields, or his miserable life with Mrs. Louise.

"Reverend Crowder! It's me, Lilly Jackson."

"Lilly Jackson? Sarah Jackson's daughter?"

"Yes, sir."

"Who's that with you?"

"That's my daughter, Iris."

"What in the world brings you two pretty women to my neck of the woods?"

"We came to ask you to do us a favor for my mama."

"Well… y'all come on in."

Lilly and Iris sat on a bench, in the hallway, while Reverend Crowder went into the kitchen. The planks on the floor were buckling from rainwater that had leaked through the ceiling. The spaces between each plank were so wide that the ground underneath the house was visible. Reverend Crowder soon returned, carrying a chair. He then sat down, in front of them, and began to converse.

"I know Sarah Jackson quite well. She's a good friend of mine. I once bought an old mule, named Sue, from her." Revered Crowder then briefly reflected before saying, "That mule meant the world to me. Even though she was deaf and blind when I bought her, I would still go out every morning to make sure she was fed and had plenty of water. She always knew when I was there. Miss Sue used to walk with me while fanning that long tail of hers… not just to shun the flies, but also to let me know that she loved me. I would rub her aching back and talk to her just like I'm talking to y'all right now. Although my sweet mule is dead, sometimes I go outside and pretend she's still there. I sure did enjoy her company."

"Reverend Crowder… I'm sorry to hear about Sue," Lilly said, recognizing his loneliness.

"It felt really good to just have something that was always happy to greet me and that loved me unconditionally," Reverend Crowder continued, still fixated on Sue.

"I understand how you feel because I just lost my mama," Lilly said.

"Sarah..." Reverend Crowder responded. "Is Sarah Jackson dead?"

"Yes, sir," Iris answered. "She died peacefully at home."

"I'm sorry to hear that," Reverend Crowder said. "Sarah was a good woman. She once gave me some good advice. I probably would've had a much better life if I had listened."

"Thank you for speaking so highly of my mama," Lilly said.

"You're welcome. I want to thank you ladies for driving all the way down here to let me know about Sarah's death."

"Reverend Crowder, we came to ask you a favor," Iris interjected. "My grandmother always told us that when she died, she wanted you to read Psalm 23 at her graveside."

"Will you do it for her?" Lilly asked.

"It would be my pleasure."

"Thank you so much," Iris responded.

"It's getting too hot out here in this hallway. You two ladies come on in the living room where it's cooler."

Lilly and Iris followed Reverend Crowder into his dingy, dusty living room. He offered them a seat on a lumpy couch that was extremely raggedy and more uncomfortable than the bench they had been sitting on. From where they were now seated, Lilly and Iris could see Mrs. Louise standing in the kitchen.

Hoping Sarah's death would end the unfortunate saga in Mrs. Louise's pathetic life, Reverend Crowder peeped into the kitchen to inform her of the sad news. However, Mrs. Louise neither responded to her husband's words nor acknowledged Lilly and Iris' loss.

Reverend Crowder then left Mrs. Louise to her solitude and sat down in his rocking chair. Mrs. Louise suddenly walked out of the back door, slamming it behind her. The silhouette of her taking sheets off the clotheslines and putting them in a basket reflected through the cracked panes of a window.

Reverend Crowder, Lilly, and Iris shared a few moments of uncomfortable silence before continuing with their prior conversation.

"Your mama loved listening to good music," Reverend Crowder said. "Will someone be there to sing?"

"Yes… Miss Carrie will be singing Amazing Grace," Lilly answered.

"Carrie Williams?" Reverend Crowder inquired, surprised.

"Yes… my grandmother specifically requested you and her," Iris replied.

"Out of respect for my good friend, Sarah… I'll be there," Reverend Crowder said, obviously still in love with Miss Carrie. "When and where will she be buried?"

"At our family graveyard," Lilly responded. "Her funeral is Saturday at one o'clock."

"We no longer live on Lane Street," Iris said.

"I know," Reverend Crowder said. "Your new home is bigger than most white folks' houses. I never expected colored folks to have such a nice place. You ladies should be very proud."

"Thank you, Reverend Crowder," Lilly said.

"We are very proud," Iris added.

Mrs. Louise walked back into the house, carrying a clothesbasket full of folded sheets. Lilly asked her how she was doing and if she would be attending Sarah's funeral. But, Mrs. Louise just walked past them without uttering a word.

"I'll be there," Reverend Crowder whispered. "Don't feel bad that Louise didn't speak to you. She hasn't spoken to me in years."

"I understand," Lilly replied.

"Now, let me see y'all to the door. You ladies better hurry home before it gets too dark. It's hard to find your way out of these woods at night."

"Thank you so much," Iris responded.

"I'll see y'all on Saturday," Reverend Crowder said, walking them to the door.

"Thanks again, Reverend Crowder," Lilly responded. She then loudly said, "Goodbye, Mrs. Louise."

The sky was beginning to cloud and it looked as though a storm was approaching. Lilly and Iris rushed to their car and quickly got inside. With their mission accomplished, they began their tiresome journey back home.

Lilly was not as talkative as she had been. Iris could sense that she was stressed and preoccupied with thoughts of Sarah's death. Perhaps this was not the best time to bombard her with questions about George Dawson, the man who had molested and impregnated her. But, Iris desperately wanted to know if the story her aunt, Rose, told her was true. Now an adult, mother, and grandmother herself—Iris felt entitled to learn more about the man who fathered her.

"You look tired," Iris said.

"I'm alright. I was just thinking about what a sad life Mrs. Louise and Reverend Crowder must live. Doesn't she know that by punishing him, she's also punishing herself? If Hell is anything like the Crowder's house, I don't want to go there!"

"I guess it's a bad time to ask you about my father."

"Even as old as I am, I still regret not asking Mama if Mr. Parker James was my father. Now, it's too late! I suppose you never get too old to want to know the truth."

"So you understand how I'm feeling?"

"Iris, I do understand. But, it's not an easy subject for me to talk about."

"When I was a little girl, Aunt Rose once told me that my father's name was George Dawson. She said that he abandoned you when you got pregnant with me?"

"That's true. I was just a young child when he got me pregnant. He did what any molester would do… fled town to avoid prosecution."

"How did he flee?"

"George escaped in the middle of the night with the assistance of Mrs. Cora Mae. Mama always hated her for hiding him out at her house and helping him skip town to avoid prosecution. We didn't see him for a while because he knew the police were searching for him."

"After I was born, did he ever come back to see you or me?"

"He once came back to Crosstown when you were about four years old. Your father was a tall, big, handsome, white-looking man. But when he reappeared—he was skinny, sickly-looking, and pale. He looked like he was knocking on death's door."

"What happened?"

"One day, Mama and I were cleaning catfish in the backyard when George just walked right up to us. He looked so different, from the healthy man we once knew, that we almost didn't recognize him. When Mama realized who he was, she told him to get the hell off of her property. George told us that he wanted to apologize for the shame he had brought to our family. He said that he was dying and was basically a dead man walking. Mama said that the world would end before any of us would offer him forgiveness. He just stood there with teary eyes, begging Mama to let him see his baby girl at least once. He even called you by your first name."

"How did he know my name?"

"I'm sure Mr. Parker James or Mrs. Cora Mae told him."

"Did Mama let him see me?"

"No way was Mama going to let George Dawson lay eyes on you! Mama told him that he would see the bowels of Hell before he would ever see her grandchild. She demanded that he immediately leave. When George could not get Mama to cooperate, he turned and pleaded with me to let him see you before he died."

"Did you let him?"

"No way could I overstep what Mama said even if I wanted to. Besides, I felt the same way about him as she did!"

"What did Mama do?"

"Mama raised the bloody butcher knife that she was using to gut catfish and pointed it directly at him! George knew that she was serious!"

"I guess he was a terrible person after all."

"I'm sorry, Iris, for saying these ugly things about your daddy, but that was the way I felt. Even after all of these years, I still feel the same way. I was just an innocent little girl and George Dawson was a fully-grown man."

"What happened next?"

"Mama told me to go into the house and to make sure you didn't wake up. And I did just that. You were still in your bed sound asleep. So I went back to the door to see what was happening."

"And then?"

"Mama finally scared George off and he left. He could barely keep his balance as he hobbled down the road towards town. Mama and I watched him until he was out of our sight."

"Did y'all ever see him again?"

"That was the last time we ever saw him. Someone told us that he went back to Texas. About three weeks later, Mr. James told us that George died from consumption. His lungs had collapsed."

"Why did Mr. James know so much about my daddy?"

"Looking back, I believe George was kin to Mr. James. Although George was much younger, he favored Mr. James enough to pass for his son. If not for Mr. James insisting that Mama let George board with us, he would never have crossed our path. But… I'm thankful our paths did cross because if they hadn't, you wouldn't have been born."

"Thank you for telling me the truth, Lilly."

"I hope you don't resent me for what I just told you. I love you with all of my heart, Iris, and Mama also loved you. I've never once regretted having you."

"I don't resent you at all. I love you and I'm proud that you're my mother. The past doesn't matter anymore. I'm at peace now. George

Dawson is dead. So let's get on with our lives. We can start right now by getting home and preparing for Mama's funeral."

"You're right, Iris! The past is done and the future belongs to us!"

CHAPTER 27

Lilly and Iris were still moping around the house for several months after Sarah's funeral. They then remembered the promise they had made to each other about living for the future and not the past. Moreover, they were certain that Sarah would have wanted them to go on with their lives. Perhaps, time does heal all wounds. Or maybe Rose Kennedy was correct when she stated, ".... The wounds remain. In time, the mind, protecting its sanity, covers them with scar tissue and the pain lessens, but it is never gone."

Eventually, Lilly and Iris would only speak of Sarah if it were something that would make them laugh. But, they never fully got over the loss of their matriarch.

Lilly and Mr. Tom Willis had even started spending a lot of time together. They shared their enjoyment of various activities such as fishing, gardening, playing cards, and taking long walks during the evenings. From an outside view, they seemed more like a married couple than just good friends.

Since Lilly had turned over complete ownership of Cleo's Place, Iris was now the sole proprietor. This kept her extremely busy. To lessen her workload, Iris was planning to partner with Bob and Rozell so they could become co-owners of the café. Their partnership would be finalized on Thanksgiving Day. To celebrate the new business endeavor, along with the holiday season, Lilly and Iris began cooking a lavish feast on the night before. Tom, Bob, and Rozell would be joining them for dinner.

Candles decorated the rosewood tables in their kitchen and dining room. The smoke from the lit candles emitted the sweet scents of cinnamon and pumpkin spices. The entire house was also filled with the aromas of roasted turkey, honey and pineapple glazed ham, crispy-fried and garlic-roasted chicken, cornbread stuffing with mushroom gravy, string beans and red potatoes, stewed rutabagas, candied yams, collard greens with fatback, oven-baked macaroni and cheese, homemade cranberry sauce, potato and ambrosia fruit salads, sweet potato pies sweetened with sorghum syrup, as well as coconut and lemon pound cakes. Jugs of sweet tea with lemons, cherry Kool-Aid, and spiked eggnog were chilled in the refrigerator. A platter with slices of cheese and a large bowl of dark purple muscadines sat on the antique coffee table in the living room.

Outside, cold winds bent tree branches and icy layers covered the ground. However, heat from the stove kept the inside of the house feeling warm and cozy.

"From the sound of that wind, it's going to be a cold winter," Lilly said.

"Yes, it sure seems that way," Iris agreed. "Do you want me to pour us a cup of that spiked eggnog?"

"I sure do. While you're getting the eggnog, hand me another jar of those string beans. To be so skinny, Tom sure can eat a lot of food."

Iris retrieved a jar of string beans and set it on the table. She then poured two cups of eggnog and handed one of them to Lilly, who took a big sip.

"I think you've been drinking without me," Iris teased. "One of the jugs of eggnog was already half empty."

"Well… a little liquor won't hurt," Lilly said, laughing. "We are adults."

When Iris removed the lid from the jar of string beans, it made a loud popping sound. The noise startled Lilly, causing her to drop the rutabaga she was peeling. They both froze with surprised expressions on their faces as they stared at each other. Then, simultaneously, they burst into uncontrollable laughter.

As Lilly emptied the string beans into a pot, Iris drank her cup of eggnog without pausing.

Suddenly, the wind blew against the windowpanes. It was so forceful that it seemed as though the glass could shatter. Iris walked over to the window and peered out into the moonlit night. She could clearly see all the way down to their family cemetery.

"Do you think we'll get some snow this winter?" Lilly asked.

"It's possible… even if it melts the same day," Iris joked. "Do you think this usually cold weather will kill our rose bushes?"

"I'll tell Tom to pile some pine straw around them. If we let those rose bushes die, Mama will come back to haunt us."

"Lilly!"

"What?"

"Nothing..."

"Nothing? You nearly scared the shit out of me for nothing!"

"I just..."

"Is someone out there?"

Iris continued to stare out of the window. She felt paralyzed and unable to move from her position. It was as if she had seen a ghost. Iris then forced herself to speak.

"Someone is standing next to Mama's grave! It looks like the shadow of a woman."

"Stop playing, Iris! You're scaring me!"

"I'm not joking! Now, she's sitting on the ground next to Mama's headstone!"

"Girl, don't you start that ghost stuff. You probably drank too much of that spiked eggnog and it's causing you to see things."

"I'm not drunk and I'm not seeing things!"

"I'm hiding the rest of that eggnog because you don't know how to hold your liquor."

"Now, she's walking away!"

"Sure… she is," Lilly said sarcastically.

"Stop making fun of me," Iris hollered. "I know what I saw!"

"Forget about what you saw, Iris. It was probably just car lights from the main road reflecting off the tree limbs."

"You're probably right."

"Let's finish cooking and get us some much needed sleep. We got company coming tomorrow for Thanksgiving dinner."

After finally preparing the last dish, Lilly and Iris stored the food away. They then went into their separate bedrooms.

Although Iris was exhausted, she could not fall asleep. The image of the ghostly woman, lurking around her grandmother's grave, was weighing heavily on her mind. Throughout the night, she either tossed and turned or stared at the ceiling.

At the first sign of dawn, Iris jumped out of her bed. She was unsure if she had really seen someone standing in their family graveyard or if the whiskey had caused her to imagine things. She was even beginning to doubt herself.

Still dressed in her nightgown, Iris put on a pair of rubber boots and a long wool coat. She quickly tied a scarf around her head before tiptoeing quietly toward the front door. Iris did not want to disturb

Lilly, who was still sound asleep. She then slowly opened the door, softly closing it behind her.

Iris hurried down the pathway toward their family cemetery. She did not notice anything out of the ordinary until something suddenly caught her attention. There was an object hanging from one of the rose bushes. Upon closer inspection, she realized it was a white lace handkerchief.

Iris was sure that it was the same handkerchief that her uncle, John, had given her grandmother, Sarah, before he was killed. Sarah had unsuccessfully searched for it when they were moving from their old dilapidated house. Iris then mumbled aloud as she reflected back to the day that her aunt, Rose, left with Mr. Charlie Sweet.

"Could this be the same lace handkerchief that my aunt was using to wipe her teary eyes? Is it possible that she has finally come back to see me?"

Iris carefully removed the delicate handkerchief from the rose thorns and placed it in her coat pocket. She then walked farther down the woody path where a nearby road led downtown. As she journeyed away from the house, soggy mud began to accumulate under her boots. Iris then noticed fresh footprints in the marshy soil.

"It wasn't a ghost after all," Iris mumbled. "The only person it could've been was my aunt, Rose! I knew, one day, she would come back to see me!"

Iris began to plead with the aunt she had not seen or heard from in several decades.

"Don't run away, again! We love you! Please, come back home!"

Iris suddenly noticed that Lilly, dressed in a robe and house shoes, was standing on the porch. Her arms were folded tightly across her chest and she was shivering from the cold. Iris had a strong urge to share what she had just found. She then surmised that there was no reason to spoil Lilly's holiday by giving her false hope that Rose had returned. Iris then decided that she would keep the lace handkerchief a secret.

Iris walked back to the house where she was greeted by Lilly.

"Good morning sunshine! Did you find your ghost?"

"No… I suppose it was just my imagination."

"Let's go back in the house before we catch pneumonia."

"I agree!"

"Our dinner guests will be here before we know it."

Iris went into her bedroom and closed the door. She took the handkerchief out of her coat pocket and gently rubbed it against her cheeks. She then placed it in her keepsake box next to the engagement ring that Sam had given her.

* * * * *

Lilly covered the dining room table with a linen tablecloth. She then arranged rose patterned china, crystal glassware, and polished silverware on top of it.

When Tom, Bob, and Rozell arrived—Iris rushed to the door and invited them inside. The guests were favorably impressed with the meal that had been prepared for them. Lilly, Iris, and Rozell were so full, after eating one serving, that they skipped dessert. However, Tom and Bob ate three platefuls before being satisfied.

After dinner, they all sat in the living room and chatted about old times.

"We sure used to have some fun nights at the café," Rozell said. "Didn't we?"

“We sure did,” Iris answered, laughing.

“Yea and I got some great target practice because of y’all fun nights,” Bob joked.

“And we’ll certainly have more memories as the years go on, especially now that we’re business partners,” Iris added.

“I noticed that some houses are being built down the road from us,” Tom said. “Who do you think our new neighbors will be?”

“I don’t know,” Lilly answered. “Hopefully it’s not any white folks.”

“Yea… let us live in peace,” Rozell said, chuckling.

“Oh… you two stop being so hateful,” Bob replied.

“Things sure have gotten much better between the blacks and whites of Crosstown,” Tom said.

“But the more things change, the more they stay the same,” Iris responded.

“I don’t care who it is as long as they’re going to get on well with the community we’ve built here on Freedom Lane,” Lilly said. “Us colored folks have to remember that we’re only as strong as our weakest link.”

After chatting away for hours, Bob and Rozell decided to go home. Iris fixed them two plates of food and a whole sweet potato pie to take with them.

Tom and Lilly then went down to the garden. They briefly conversed about their budding relationship as Tom determined if straw should be piled around the roots of the rose bushes. However, they did not remain outside long because it was getting much later and it was extremely cold. Before walking home, Tom promised Lilly that he would return tomorrow.

When Lilly came back inside the house, she and Iris sat at the kitchen table and drank a cup of coffee.

"Did Tom get home safely?" Iris asked.

"Yes," Lilly responded. "We checked the rose bushes and talked for a few moments before I came back inside."

"He seems smitten with you."

"Well… he did tell me that he had fallen in love with me."

"Really? Lilly… that's terrific!"

"He also asked me to marry him and move into his house."

"What did you say?"

"I told him that I loved him, but that I didn't want to get married."

CHAPTER 28

As Iris was walking from the creek, a shooting star streaked across the evening sky. She closed her eyes and wished that Samantha would one day find her way back home. Nevertheless—many holidays, birthdays, anniversaries, and even deaths would come and go before her wish could ever come true.

Iris occupied her days with simple things like swinging back and forth on the porch, sitting in Sarah's rocking chair while reading old letters, tending to her gardens, and reliving memories of her one and only love, Sam. The café, Cleo's Place, had long since been sold to Bob and Rozell, who were now the sole owners. Lilly and Mr. Tom Willis had cohabited for several years, enjoying a wonderful life together, until Lilly unexpectedly died peacefully in her sleep. Six months after Lilly's death, Mr. Tom died of a broken heart.

After years of having Lilly as not only her mother, but as a confidant and liaison, Iris was now alone. She was left with only the memories of the great times they once shared and occasional musings of what could have been. Even though Iris was certain that Rose and Cleo also dead, she would still occasionally think of them.

On one of those days when Iris was engulfed in her thoughts, she heard a knock at the door. Iris peaked out of her living room window and saw that it was the mailman, Mr. Edward Cooper. She started to pretend that she was not home. However, for some inexplicable reason, she changed her mind. Iris then opened the door and greeted him.

"Yes, Mr. Cooper?"

"Here's your mail, Miss Iris."

"You could've just left it in the mailbox."

"I have a special delivery that requires your signature."

As Iris glanced down at the letter, she noticed that it was from Belinda. Her hands began to tremble as she reached for it. As she signed her name on the delivery pad, Mr. Cooper seemed friendlier than his usual aloof demeanor.

"Miss Iris... it's pretty hot out here today. I was wondering if you had something cold to drink?"

"I have a pitcher of ice-cold lemonade in the refrigerator. Come on inside and I'll pour you a glass."

"That sounds great, Miss Iris."

Mr. Cooper was a tall, handsome, white man. His skin was very pale and his blue eyes sparkled. His hair was graying and his beard was well groomed. Even though Iris had seen Mr. Cooper several times before as he delivered mail, this was the first time he had ever been inside her house.

"You can have a seat at the table, Mr. Cooper."

"You have a very nice house."

"Thank you."

Mr. Cooper laid his mailbag against the wall and sat down at the table. Iris took a pitcher of lemonade out of the refrigerator and set it in front of him. She then poured him a full glass, accidently spilling a little onto the tablecloth. As she cleaned it up with a towel, she noticed that Mr. Cooper was admiring her round hips and firm silhouette that showed through her housedress. Pretending not to notice his subtle flirting, Iris placed a cookie jar of teacakes on the table before sitting across from him.

"Make yourself at home, Mr. Cooper."

"Thank you, Miss Iris. I'll do just that."

As Mr. Cooper drank lemonade and ate teacakes, Iris opened Belinda's letter and silently read it to herself.

My Dearest Iris,

I hope this letter finds you happy and well. I didn't think I would ever say this, but I'm ready to move back to Crosstown. I'm tired of the big city life. As I get older, I long for the peace and quiet of the country.

I heard about Miss Sarah and Lilly's death. You and I have lost some special people in our lives. I don't know if you heard, but Mrs. Cora Mae recently passed. My mama also died, about five years ago, and I had her body cremated. I still keep her ashes in a beautiful urn that sits on my shelf. I want to bring her ashes home so she can be buried next to daddy, Sam, Miss Sarah, and Lilly.

But this time when I come home, I won't be leaving! Iris, you are now the only family I have left. I want us to reconnect and be best friends just like we used to be.

I miss you so much and I can't wait to see you!

P.S. I also have a huge surprise for you! Let's just say... I'm not the only person who'll be moving back to Crosstown!

Love,

Belinda

As Mr. Cooper poured himself another glass of lemonade, Iris excused herself from the table and went into her bedroom. She took a pen and writing pad from her dresser. She then sat on top of her four-poster bed before quickly writing a short reply.

My Dearest Belinda,

Bring your mother's remains home and bury her among the fam-

ily that always loved her and on the land where she once lived.

I've missed you and your friendship. Time has separated us long enough. Please, hurry home!

P.S. I can't wait to discover the identity of your surprise! It would be so nice if it were my long lost friend, Annie! Seeing you both again would be a dream come true!

Sincerely,

Iris

"Miss Iris, thanks for the lemonade and tea cakes, but I must get going."

"I'll be right there, Mr. Cooper."

Iris quickly addressed an envelope to Belinda and sealed the letter inside. She took a dime from the loose change that was on top of her vanity to give to Mr. Cooper for a stamp.

When Iris returned from her bedroom, Mr. Cooper was standing at the front door. She handed him the envelope and dime. Mr. Cooper put the dime in his pocket and the letter in his mailbag.

"Thanks again for the lemonade and teacakes."

"You're welcome, Mr. Cooper. Come back anytime."

"Well, I'll remember that." As Mr. Cooper walked onto the porch, he turned around and said, "Miss Iris… would you mind if I stopped by to visit you on the weekends?"

"I would love that Mr. Cooper," Iris responded with a slight smile.

Iris then stood on her porch and watched Mr. Cooper wipe the sweat from his brow onto the sleeves of his blue shirt as he journeyed on his route.

Iris also wiped sweat from her forehead. For the first time in years, she felt beautiful and as though she could love another man again. But what would her future hold? Was her attraction to Mr. Cooper pure loneliness or the beginning of a new chapter? Is his whiteness an insignificant factor or a contradiction to her hopes that her long-lost daughter, Samantha, would someday return to her roots? As Iris contemplated those questions, she whispered, “It’s going to be one long, hot summer!”

WE HOPE YOU ENJOYED READING *BREAKING THE CHAIN*….

Turn the pages to learn more about some of our other publications and how to contact us!

BROKEN PROMISES

A PLAY BY FRANKIE BERRY WISE

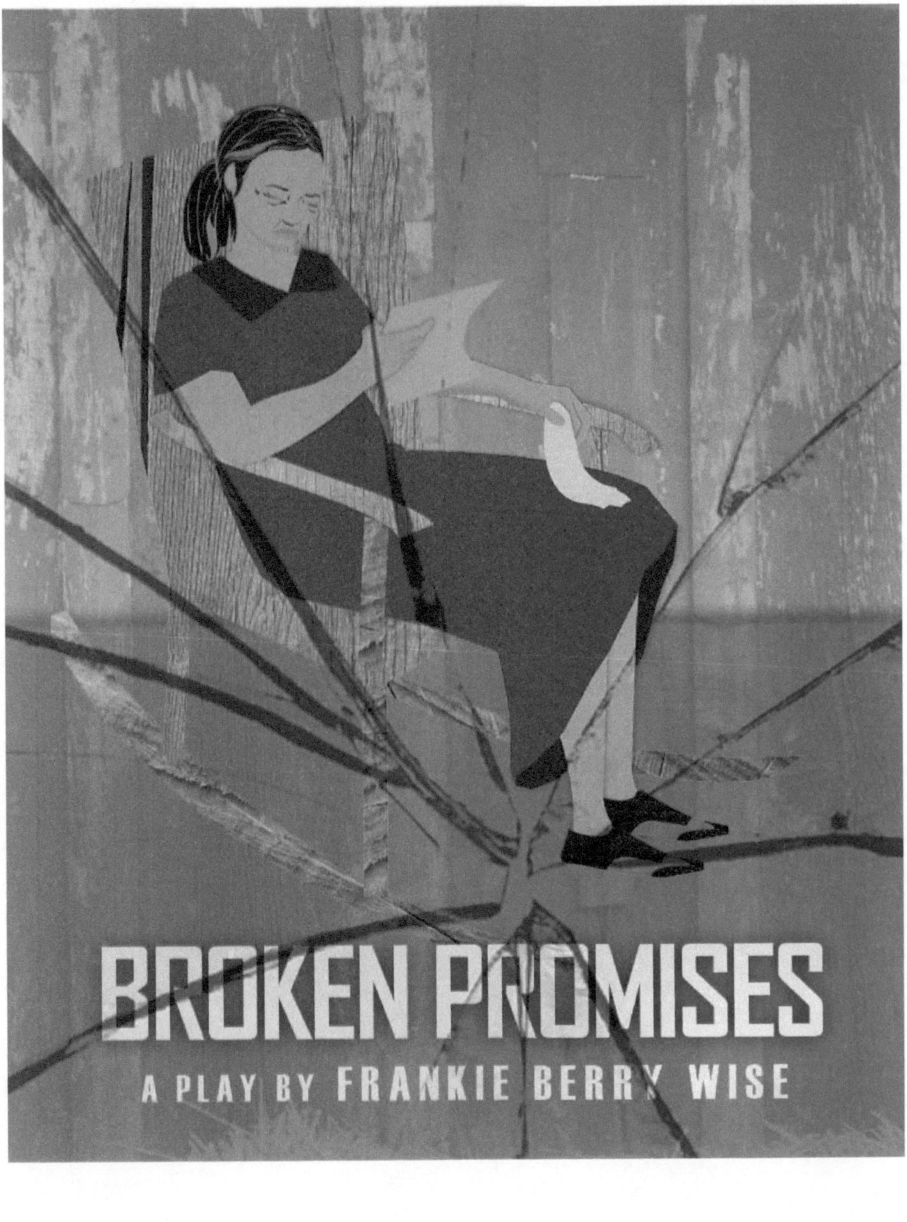

EXIT

FRANKIE BERRY WISE

FRANKIE BERRY WISE

EXIT

A HEART-WRENCHING MYSTERY

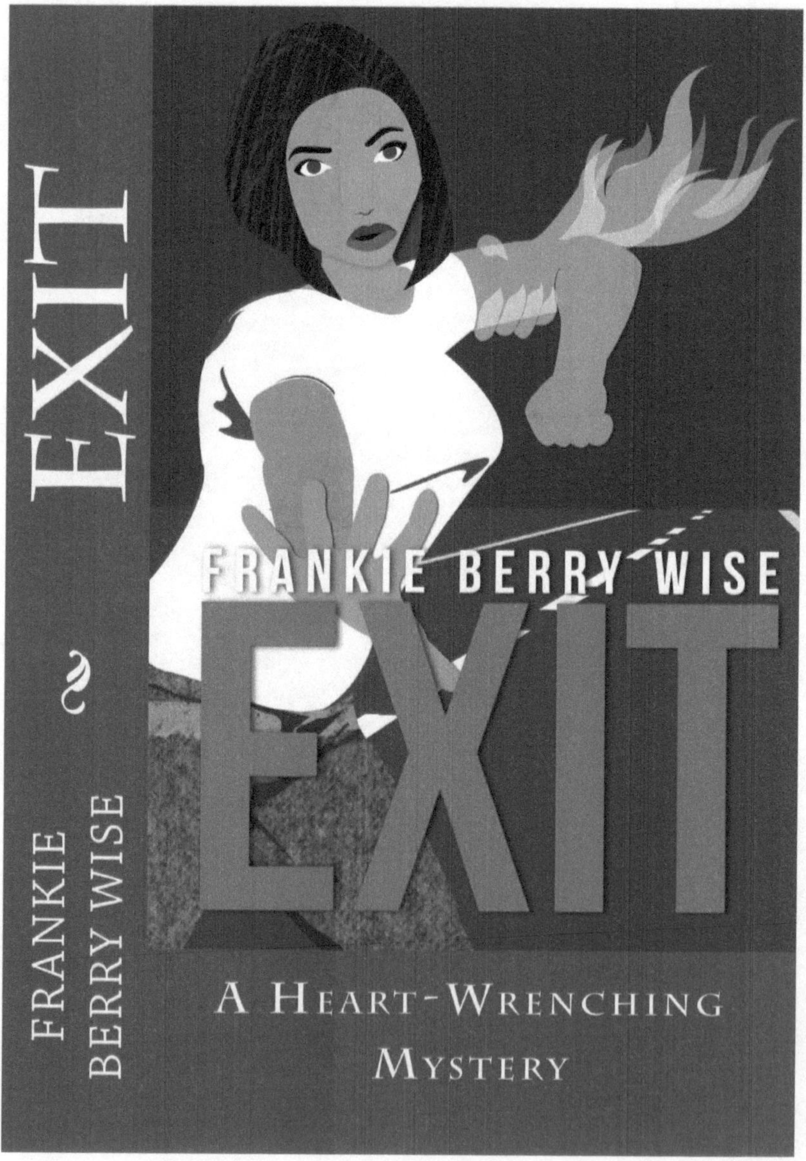

CONTACT US

www.wisescholarspublishing.com

www.facebook.com/wisescholarspublishing

wisescholarspublishing

@marshalettewise

marshalette@wisescholarspublishing.com

1-888-735-6392

1-334-452-4596 (Fax)

www.ingramcontent.com/pod-product-compliance
Lightning Source LLC
Chambersburg PA
CBHW030412310726
48979CB00002B/380

* 9 7 8 0 9 9 6 3 9 4 6 1 1 *